PENALTY KILL

UTAH FURY HOCKEY BOOK TEN

BRITTNEY MULLINER

PENALTY KILL

ALSO BY BRITTNEY MULLINER

ROMANCE

Utah Fury Hockey

Puck Drop (Reese and Chloe)

Match Penalty (Erik and Madeline)

Line Change (Noah and Colby)

Attaching Zone (Wyatt and Kendall)

Buzzer Beater (Colin and Lucy)

Open Net (Olli and Emma)

Full Strength (Grant and Addison)

Drop Pass (Nikolay and Elena)

Scoring Chance (Derrek and Amelia)

Penalty Kill (Brandon and Sydney)

Power Play (Jason and Taylor)

Center Ice (Jake and Dani)

Game Misconduct (Parker and Vivian)

Face Off (Mikey and Holly)

Snowflakes & Ice Skates (Lance and Jessica)

A Holiday Short Story to be read between Center Ice and Game Misconduct

West Penn Hockey

Cheat Shot

Trick Play

Enemy Games

Fake Assist

Royals of Lochland

His Royal Request

His Royal Regret

Her Royal Rebellion

Young Adult

No Regrets Series

Ask No Questions

Tell No Lies

Make No Mistake

Charmed Series

Finding My Charming

Finding My Forever

Standalones

The Invisibles

For exclusive content and the most up to date news, sign up for
Brittney's Reader's club here

PENALTY KILL

The period from which a team becomes short-handed due to one or more penalties until they are at full or even strength with the opposing team. Also refers to the defensive activity during such a period. The disadvantaged team is basically "killing" the penalty by denying the opposing team the opportunity to score when they have the upper hand.

https://www.sportingcharts.com/dictionary/nhl/penalty-kill.aspx

1

BRANDON

"You can't do this again, Olivia. You promised the boys." I nearly threw my phone against the wall, but this was already my second one this month. I couldn't let her get to me. It was what she wanted.

"I can't change the photoshoot. They'll understand."

"You really think they'll understand why their mom isn't here. Again. They're four."

"It's a preschool graduation. It's not even a real thing." She sighed. "They'll appreciate all my hard work when they're older. I'm doing this for them."

"Oh really? That's how you're justifying things? How is any of this for them?"

"Because when they grow up they'll know that women can do anything. They'll be respectful and supportive of women."

"I can teach them that. What I can't do is be their mom. They miss you." I didn't know why exactly. She wasn't exactly the type of mom to create great memories with her children.

"I miss them too. Terribly. Tell them I'll call them later."

She hung up and I dropped into the nearest chair. How

I'd ever loved that woman was a mystery. She was selfish and cruel, but she hadn't always been that way. When we met in college, she was shy and focused on excelling so she could one day change the world as a doctor. We got married the summer before our senior year. We were young, idealistic, and so in love. I should have seen sooner how much she'd changed from when we met. It was all there before we said "I do," but I was blind. My family knew. My friends knew. Even my coaches knew, but none of them thought to say something before we sealed our fates together forever.

After the wedding, she changed her major from pre-med to public health. She said she didn't want such a demanding career anymore. She wanted to be home with our children.

What she really meant was she saw the attention I was getting from the NHL. The chatter about me being a first-round draft pick. She saw a future, an easier one than she had planned, and took it.

I thought she loved me and wanted us to be a family.

She wanted fame and fortune. When I was drafted by the Utah Fury thirteen years ago, she immediately emersed herself in all the attention she could get. She used me, and now I knew better than to ever trust a woman like that again.

"Boys, are you dressed?" I called out knowing they were probably still playing together in their room. I'd asked them at least four times to get ready for preschool, but I was easy to ignore when they were in dinosaur playing mode.

They'd picked up on the changes in our family despite my attempts to keep things as normal as possible. They knew their mom was gone. I told them she would be back to visit and they would see her soon, but somehow at four years old, they were smarter than me. They knew the truth. She'd never been very involved with them. Sure, the twins looked cute on her social media accounts, but other than a few overly staged pictures, she didn't take notice of them. The boys were simply props to use in her effort to show the world how perfect her life was.

That's where she was now. Living her best life. At least that was the hashtag she kept using. She left Salt Lake and took off to live in Malibu with her two best friends so they could continue to build her brand. She was a model now. An influencer. Whatever that meant. All I knew was she was no longer a role model for her boys. She had no influence over them. The two people that should matter to her more than anything else in the world were at the bottom of her priority list.

At this point, I was fine being forgotten, replaced by the attention and love she gained from her online followers. I didn't care, as long as the boys were happy.

Nearly a year ago, when I came home from a five-day road trip with the team, exhausted and beat up, to find the boys alone in the house crying, I lost my mind. She said she'd only left them alone for a few minutes, but I knew from tracking her phone that she'd been gone for hours. Inspiration had struck for a new post and she just had to go get her shot. She hadn't bothered calling for a sitter. Nope. She'd been so focused, so in the zone, that she'd forgotten I wasn't home and they would be alone.

That was the day I told her to figure out her priorities or leave.

She took her chance, told me her calling was in Hollywood, and left.

The divorce papers I filed followed her.

Thank heaven my parents had been smarter than me. They knew where my career was headed and they saw through Olivia in ways I never did. They made sure we had a prenup in place. I owed her nothing more than the gifts I'd purchased for her over the years. I let her keep her car as well. She didn't want custody of the boys, just three weeks each summer. *If* it worked around her schedule. That blew my mind, but shouldn't have surprised me. She said she didn't have time to be a mother right now. She needed to focus on her. Like that was any different from the last four years.

I stood and rubbed my face as I walked down the hall to the boys' room. I leaned against the doorframe and frowned. "Boys. I told you to get dressed."

Their two blond heads popped up from on top of Milo's bed.

"But *Dad*," Finn whined.

"We're already late. Please get dressed." I pointed at the clothes I set out for them at the bottom of their ladders.

With overdramatic shoulder drops and sighs, they climbed down and Finn marched across the room. Painfully, so painfully slowly, they got changed before dragging their feet behind me and down the stairs.

I was going to be late for practice, again, but they didn't care. No one seemed to. My agent, the coaches, the guys. No one said anything when I was the last one on the ice, minutes after I should be. It was like they all agreed to give me a pass. I wasn't sure how long it would last, and as grateful as I was for their understanding, I hated it. It felt like pity.

Unfortunately, I needed it. I needed them to turn a blind eye to my slip-ups. I needed some leeway while I fought to keep my head above water. Olivia had been in California for eight months and before she left, I'd never been on my own with the boys. Since the moment they were born, people— family, friends, and Olivia's entourage—were always there.

Now, I was all they had. I was responsible for feeding them. Bathing them. Getting them to preschool. Keeping them alive and trying my absolute best to create a sense of normalcy and routine. Kids were resilient, and Milo and Finn never once complained about the changes, but I felt like I was failing them.

They needed, no they deserved, two functioning, dedicated parents. What they had was a professional athlete for a father, one who never had enough time in the day. If money could solve everything, we wouldn't have any issues, but that was so far from the truth. Money had done nothing but make it easy for Olivia to ignore her children and abandon her family.

"Remember today is the long day. I'll be there later than normal to pick you guys up."

Finn didn't react to my reminder, but Milo pouted. "I don't like long days."

I felt bad having to keep them at their preschool for additional hours so I could be at practice and the team workout, but I didn't have a choice.

"I know, bud."

We passed through the kitchen and I grabbed the boys' lunch boxes off the counter where I left them. It was something I'd only recently learned how to do. I was dropping them off at preschool for two months before their teacher finally called me and told me they needed to bring their own lunches. She was fine providing food when a child forgot, but since it was becoming a trend, she was worried.

What kind of father forgot to provide food for his kids? The kind that didn't know. As much as I wanted to blame Olivia for everything that happened, I knew I shared the blame. I let my home life go on autopilot. Other people cleaned the house. My personal assistant ran most of my life behind the scenes. Taking care of things before I even realized I needed it done. I was so far removed, I didn't know my boys needed lunch.

That was the wakeup call I needed. I had to do better. The boys deserved better. I couldn't cut back at work. My team required me at my best. I might not be one of the cool, young guys, but I was a great centerman and one of the top scorers on the team. Those guys were my family too. All I had to do was relearn. Regroup. I could do better, be who everyone needed me to be, but things had to change. There were other guys on the team who managed being a player, father, and more. I knew it was possible. I just needed a chance to catch up.

"In the car, guys." They ran out the door, ducking under my arm.

I helped Milo buckle his booster seat before checking on Finn. Once they were both ready, I got in and drove the ten minutes to their preschool. They sang along to a really horrible cover of nursery rhymes sung by other children. I hated the music, but it was their favorite. Another gift from my ex.

I could be a single parent. I just needed to figure out how. I also needed to find help. Pride wasn't something I struggled with. I was more than willing to admit that I was out of my element and needed help. I knew plenty of people who could do this on their own. They could be everything the boys needed, but I wasn't one of them. It wasn't something I could ask my assistant to help out with. He was already running my errands and managing my schedule. To ask for more help would be inappropriate. Plus, he wasn't a kid person. He avoided the boys when he was at the house. It was fine. Not everyone loves children, and I wouldn't force him.

"Daddy, did you get our green?" Finn blurted over the music. I turned it down while trying to decipher what he meant.

"What green?" I watched them look at each other in exasperation and I almost laughed. Such mature frustration for little humans.

"We have to wear green for St. Patrick's Day," Milo reminded me.

Right. Of course. They came home with a flyer last week to tell parents about the class's celebration. I managed to avoid being responsible for food or volunteering but the boys were adamant that they needed new green shirts. None of the five in their closets was sufficient.

It was two days away. I had plenty of time to find something green, between practice, team workout, tomorrow's warm-up, and the game. Sure, I would find time to get to a store. Just as soon as I figured out a way to clone myself.

"I'm getting them today."

"I don't want the same as Milo," Finn whined.

"I will get you guys different ones, don't worry." They were in an independent phase at the moment. They refused to wear anything remotely similar to the other. Last month, they wanted to match and even have their hair cut the same so everyone would know they were twins.

Their flip-flopping was more than I could keep up with. I didn't try. I just waited for them to tell me each day what mood they were in.

I pulled in front of their preschool and the boys began unbuckling themselves. I got out and said, "Okay, guys, I'll see you later. Be good for your teachers."

They nodded as they jumped out of the car. Finn paused to hug me but Milo ran past. As much as I tried to not let it get to me, I grew more worried each day that passed without him reaching out for me.

"Bye, Dad!" they called back as they worked together to pull open the door. I waited until I could see them walk into their classroom before getting back in the car. I had twenty minutes before practice. That was exactly enough time to get to the arena and dress out. I couldn't go shopping, but the boys would be sad if I was any later to pick them up than usual.

I blew out a breath and turned back onto the street. I only had one option.

"Hey, Brandon." Emma's voice filled the car.

"Hey Em. How's it going?"

I heard quiet cries and frowned. She had enough going on. I shouldn't have called.

"Pretty good. Jackson's teething, but we're surviving."

"Good. Good."

"Brandon, what do you need?" I could hear the smile in her voice. Emma and Olli had been good friends to me when my life flipped upside down. She gathered the women from the Pride to step in and babysit when I needed it. She was my main resource for advice and questions with the boys. Even though Jackson was still less than a year old, she knew more than I did. Mothering came so naturally to her. She was my saving grace.

"The boys want new green shirts for their class's St. Patrick's Day celebration."

"Okay. I'm heading to the mall downtown today, so I'll pick up something for them."

I let out a sigh. "Are you sure it's not an inconvenience?"

She was always so good about fitting my requests into her normal day. Whether it was the grocery store, craft supplies, the bakery the boys love, or the mall, she always happened to be going the day I needed her help. She was wonderful. One day I'd find a way to repay her and the rest of the Pride for helping me without making me feel like the failure I was.

"Not at all. I'm meeting Chloe to do some baby shopping, so we'll be at kid stores all day."

"Thank you, Emma. Really."

"No problem."

I was about to hang up when I remembered Finn's request.

"Oh, and they want different shirts. No matching."

"I know. Milo told me last week that they were sick of getting mixed up."

Of course, she already knew.

"Thank you." I shook my head as I pulled into the underground parking beneath the arena.

"I'll drop them by the house later today. Bye, Brandon."

Great, one thing off my mind. Just a thousand other things to figure out and sort through. Not for the next few hours though. The moment I stepped out of the car, I was no longer Dad. I was Cullen. Number twenty-one.

Nonstop days like today made me feel the difference between those two more than ever. Just another thing to worry about later.

2

SYDNEY

I set the stack of applications on the café table in front of me and picked up my tea. This was day four of pounding the pavement and searching for a job. Salt Lake seemed more promising than Denver when I first decided to move, but I wasn't having any luck. I wasn't worried quite yet. I had enough money left to last me another week.

I wasn't at Michigan-desperation level and hopefully, I would never let myself get to that point again. As much as I appreciated the women's shelter in Lansing letting me in during the middle of winter three years ago, I knew better than to end up back in that situation. I felt guilty using resources that could have helped another woman, one without options, but I'd had to move on from Columbus so fast. Too fast to set up a new job or apartment in Lansing. My landlord in Columbus had hit on me multiple times in the three months I lived there, but one night he threatened to evict me if I didn't let him in to 'get to know each other.' He'd given off bad vibes since I moved in, and I decided not to take any chances. I disappeared that night and headed for Michigan without a plan.

Since then, I'd kept enough money on hand to last me two weeks without a job. It was enough to keep me from panicking, but not enough to let me get complacent.

There were a few stores hiring at the outdoor mall downtown, but retail wasn't my number one choice. I'd been a receptionist in Cincinnati and Newport. That was my favorite position I'd had so far. Well, selling ice cream on the Jersey Shore was pretty fun, but not so great for my bank account.

A couple of women walked past me, and I scooted in so they could get by to the sitting area next to my table. They spoke quickly to one another, and the blond barista with wild ringlets at the counter was shouting to stay in the conversation.

I looked around the small café and realized I was the only other customer. People must have cleared away while I filled out the endless paperwork in front of me.

"No, I really am worried about him now." A cheerful, honey-blond woman shook her head at the barista. "This has been going on longer than any of us thought."

A beautiful brunette leaned back in her chair and set her feet up on the coffee table. She rubbed her pregnant belly and sighed. "Telling him isn't going to convince him. You know how stubborn they all are. It needs to be his idea."

"I don't think he's all that stubborn. He's drowning right now." The honey-blond said as she pulled an adorable baby out of a car seat and sat him on her lap. "If he's to the point of calling us for help, he's past holding on to any pride or ego. He just doesn't know what he needs."

"Which is what?" The barista came from behind the counter and sat on the edge of the brunette's chair.

I knew I was shamelessly eavesdropping, but their dynamic was intriguing. They seemed to know each other really well and were able to leave things unspoken, yet they all understood one another. What would it be like to have friends like that? To be a part of a group that close?

"He needs a full-time nanny. Someone who can be there for the boys and run errands for them and make sure things don't slip through the cracks." Honey—I decided to give the blond a nickname—told the others.

"Can't his assistant do that?" Barista asked.

My eyes bounced around to each of them hoping to be clued in with more information. Who were they talking about? What did a person have to do to have an assistant? Some fancy corporate boss, probably. Why couldn't he take care of the boys? Where was Mr. Fancy's wife?

"He's got enough on his plate," Brunette answered. "You're right, Emma. He needs a nanny."

So, Honey's name was Emma. I watched her and smiled. She looked like an Emma, sweet and caring.

"Do any of you know someone?" Emma asked the other two.

Brunette shook her head. "Not really my area of expertise." She rubbed her belly. "At least not yet."

Barista sat up. "Addison might know someone."

"I'll have to ask her later," Emma replied while looking down at the boy in her lap. "Maybe I should find a few options first and vet them before bringing it up to Brandon. It would probably be less overwhelming that way."

"Definitely. Always present the solution with the problem," Brunette said with a confident nod.

I stared down at my pile of applications. I really didn't want to go back to working retail. As an only child, I didn't have a ton experience with kids, but I was the babysitter in my neighborhood in high school and for people I met over the years. It wasn't like I was completely inept. I could do it.

I picked up the top application and stood. I turned to the women and waited for them to notice me. Brunette sized me up with a raised eyebrow while Barista gave me a small smile. Emma was the only one to speak.

"Hi. Sorry, were we being too loud? We didn't mean to bother you."

"Actually, I'm looking for a job." I held out the application. "I'm new to the area and have been filling out applications for the past few days. I couldn't help but overhear that you're looking for a nanny. I have plenty of babysitting experience, and my previous jobs and references are all on there."

Slowly, she reached out and took the paper from me. She looked it over with a gentle smile. "Do you believe in fate, Sydney Banks?"

I nodded. "Actually, yes. I do."

Her eyes found mine. "Me too."

Brunette turned in her seat to face me. "Have you ever nannied before?"

"No," I answered honestly. She seemed like the type to get straight to the point. "I've babysat quite a bit, and I was an administrative assistant before so I know how to manage a schedule, run errands, and keep an office running. I'm sure the principles can be easily applied to nannying."

She eyed me before nodding.

"Have you ever worked for anyone..." Barista trailed off and looked at her friends before returning to me. "High profile?"

I was right. This was for some fancy pants CEO or something. I wasn't sure who was famous in Salt Lake, so I simply nodded. "Yes, I understand the need to be discrete."

"It's not so much that." Emma laughed. "It's just that his life can be demanding. Weird hours and there would probably be some unique requests."

For the first time, I was beginning to doubt my quick decision. Why were they making it sound so sketchy? Like I'd be doing some questionable things?

"I'm sure I can handle it." I hoped I sounded more confident than I felt.

"I'm sure you can," Brunette said with a sly smile. "We'll reach out to your references."

Emma nodded and smiled at me, and I took that as my dismissal. "Thanks."

I returned to my table and picked up my purse and applications. I felt a little unhinged for approaching a bunch of strangers, but I didn't regret taking a chance. The worst thing that could happen was that I never hear from them again.

I was almost to the door when one of them called my name.

I spun to see Brunette hurrying toward me. "Are you single?"

The question caught me off guard. Was... was she hitting on me? "Um, yes."

She nodded. "That's good."

I was about to ask her why she needed to know, but she turned around and walked back to her group without another word.

Well, that just made the whole experience even weirder. Maybe I didn't want the position. They'd done a great job of freaking me out.

I looked at my completed applications as I walked down the sidewalk. It was time to turn these in.

I had just walked into my motel room that smelled like bleach and stale smoke when my phone rang with a number I didn't know. It was a Salt Lake area code, so I answered in case it was about a job.

"This is Sydney."

"You've moved around quite a bit. Why?" I vaguely recognized the voice, but the personal question caught me off guard.

"I'm sorry, who is this?"

"Chloe Murray. We met at the café this afternoon."

Ah, the intimidating brunette; that's where I knew her voice. "I enjoy traveling and experiencing new cities. I don't have anything to tie me down."

"It seems like you stay in each place for six to eight months. Is that how long we can expect you to stay this time?"

This was a job interview. I could feel it. "It depends." It was the best answer I could give her. I'd moved so much because I hadn't found what I was looking for. A place worth staying. My wanderlust was too strong. The innate desire to keep moving propelled me from city to city.

"We would like a commitment of at least a year from whoever would be filling the position. The boys have had too much change recently. They need stability."

A year. In Salt Lake. Did I want that?

There was no way of knowing until I settled in.

Emma's question from the café ran through my mind. I did believe in fate. There were too many coincidences in life to ignore that there just might be an outside force pushing people together with perfect timing. I had to trust that this was one of those times.

"I've never found a place I wanted to stay for more than a few months. I'm hoping Salt Lake is different."

She hummed. I doubted that telling her a palm reader on Bourbon Street told me I'd find my place near the salty lake would reassure her. She probably thought I was strange enough for walking up to them in the first place. Then again, she was calling. That was a good sign.

"I'm going to need a little more than you hope it works out here. Can you commit to a year-long contract or not?"

I was on the spot, but the idea of dealing with ornery

retail customers all day was enough to push me over the edge. "Yes, I can."

"Good. Your references had nothing but glowing praise to give. It was impressive enough to intrigue me despite your resume looking somewhat... uncommitted. I'd like you to meet Brandon and the boys on Thursday at eleven. Will that work?"

That gave me two days to prepare myself. "Sure."

"Perfect. I'll text you the address."

"Sounds good."

"Bye, Sydney."

She hung up before I could reply. She didn't seem the type to mess around, so she must have called my references if she trusted me enough to offer a position. I sat on the edge of the lumpy bed and looked around. Hopefully Mr. Fancy Pants liked me. I guess it was probably more important that his children did, and that I liked them.

A whole year. In one place.

Were the walls closing in on me, or was that my imagination?

The last time I'd stayed in a city that long was before I left my parents' house at eighteen. I'd been on the move since the day after high school graduation. I couldn't stand the thought of living in the same town my parents, grandparents, and great-grandparents had called home. I needed out. I needed my own life. Three generations of never leaving, and they expected me to be the fourth. West Huntburgh, Pennsylvania had been enough for them. No vacations or road trips, other than the annual trip to the family cabin at Lake Erie just two hours away. But it was one boring house in a boring town to another.

My parents didn't understand my need to leave. They said I was ungrateful for all they provided for me. Their lives were fulfilling for them, so following in their footsteps should be the same for me.

The itch to get out and see the world set in during eighth grade geography class when I realized how much I was missing. I dreamed of seeing it all. Paris, Rio, Hong Kong. I wanted to travel the world and experience what other countries and cultures had to offer. Unfortunately, you needed money to travel, especially internationally, and I couldn't even afford a passport when I first left. I started off with Philadelphia. It was only a few hours from my hometown, but it might as well have been the moon. In the ten years since I left, I've lived in nearly every state, but I still haven't managed to leave the country. I haven't been able to build up enough of a savings to feel secure about taking that leap.

Staying here wasn't a setback.

I'd have to remind myself of that every day. I wasn't sure what the pay was, but nannies could make good money, especially for rich people. This could be my big break. I'd save up for the whole year and it might be enough to get a passport and a one-way ticket to explore the world.

3

BRANDON

This was insane. I was crazy for letting Chloe and Emma talk me into it. Not that *anyone* was capable of saying no to those two, not when their minds were set on something. I wiped my hands on my jeans for the third time. Why was I so nervous? It wasn't like I was the one walking into a job interview.

My knee bounced a mile a minute while I watched the boys race each other up the stairs to the highest slide at the park. They were fearless. I was pretty sure they were supposed to be playing on the little kids' playground still, but telling them to stick to that side was an insult to their egos. That was for babies, apparently. They were big boys and could handle the *real* playground. Sure, they were ready, but I wasn't. It was easy to lose sight of them. They were too fast and too brave for their own good. The two of them fed off one another, pushing each other to take more risks, showing off that they weren't scared.

It was terrifying.

I checked my watch and sighed. I thought it would be a good idea to get here early so the boys could burn off some of their energy before the woman Chloe interviewed got here. I didn't want to scare her off before I had a chance to talk to her, but my idea might have backfired. The boys were screaming, chasing, and at a full-on energy level ten with no sign of slowing down.

There weren't very many other kids here either, so it wasn't like I could distract her from noticing which children were mine. It was hard to miss the two towheads blitzing from one side of the playset to the other while screaming at the top of their lungs.

"Brandon?"

I turned to see a beautiful woman walking toward me. Her long caramel hair nearly touched her hips. Her skin seemed to be glowing. She was wearing flowy, turquoise floral pants and a baggy yellow shirt tied around her waist. I tried to look away from the thin strip of tan skin peeking through the gap between her top and pants, but it was hypnotizing. A hippie goddess.

I shook my head. *Bad Brandon.* It had been a while—years —since I'd noticed a woman this way. It was such a foreign feeling it took me a while to identify it as attraction, so long that the beautiful woman was now staring at me with an uncertain expression.

"Sorry, my mistake. I'm looking for someone, but I don't know what he looks like." She turned and started walking away, and I realized I needed to respond. Two minutes ago.

"Yes, I'm Brandon." She faced me, not looking convinced. I guess I would be confused too. "Sydney, right?"

She grinned, making her hazel eyes sparkle, and moved to the bench I was sitting on. She offered her hand, and I shook it quickly before she sat down. "I'm so glad I found you. All Chloe told me was to look for a man with brown hair."

I chuckled. "I guess she could have done a bit more to help you out."

She laughed lightly, a delicate sound that had me wanting to lean in. I had to stop myself from scooting closer. "Thanks for agreeing to meet me. I can only imagine how weird it must be for a complete stranger to want to watch your children."

Weird? No, it was an answer to a prayer. I didn't want her to know how desperate I was for help. I didn't even fight it when Emma and Chloe presented me with the idea after practice on Tuesday. I hugged them when they said that not only did they think I needed a nanny, but they had a woman in mind. It was exactly what I didn't know I needed. I knew I couldn't do this on my own. The boys were suffering from my limited time, which wasn't fair. If I could find the right fit for us, this would solve so much. If Sydney could care for them, they would get some of the much-needed attention and focus they deserved. I knew there was no replacement for their mother, but having someone in their life that they could depend on? That was the best I could give them at the moment. Things would slow down a bit once the season ended, but that was months away. Sydney could be there for them now.

As long as I didn't scare her away.

"I really appreciate it. I'm not sure how much the women told you, but I'm new to the world of single parenting and need help." I tried to smile but it fell flat. "I've let the ball drop with the boys too many times recently, and I've accepted that we need help."

She chuckled. "Well, that is the first step."

I laughed and the corners of her eyes crinkled. I loved it.

Wait. No. I can't feel anything. Not for her. She was a potential nanny, not someone for me to flirt with.

"Right." I cleared my throat. "Milo and Finn are four. They go to preschool for four hours a day, and three times a week they stay for another two to three hours in the daycare program. I'm hoping having a nanny will make it so they don't have to do that anymore. I'd rather have them home or at the park or something." I shrugged.

She nodded. "I understand. Emma and Chloe also mentioned you need someone to keep up with their schedule and errands."

I winced. "Yeah, I feel like I'm losing my mind most of the time. I can't seem to remember when it's their turn to bring treats at school or when they're supposed to dress up for a holiday or spirit day." I looked over to check on the boys before meeting her eyes again. "Unfortunately, I can't stay on top of it all. Not right now."

I waited to see the judgment on her face, but it never came. She just smiled. "I can't pretend to know what you're going through, but I--"

She paused for a second before jumping up.

I watched her, confused as she took off running across the sandy playground. I scanned the area for the boys but didn't see them. I followed her until I realized where she was headed. Milo managed to climb to the top of the monkey bars and was stuck between the first and second rod. He was barely holding on by one hand and one stuck foot. It was at least a twelve-foot drop. My heart was in my throat as I ran to him.

Sydney got to the steps and reached up for him, pulling him into her chest. She got back to the ground and knelt so she could stand him up. He whimpered and Finn mirrored his brother's emotions. They were both terrified when I reached them.

"You're okay. I know that was scary, but you're okay now," Sydney spoke in a calm voice.

"Milo, why were you up there?" I tried to keep my tone level, but concern and anger washed over me. "You know better than that."

Milo and Finn blinked up at me with watery eyes. "I'm sorry." They cried at the same time.

"These are your boys?" Sydney asked.

I nodded and then realized she took off running for a

random child. She didn't know beforehand she was saving my son. I didn't need to know anything else about her. She demonstrated the type of person she was more than words ever could.

"Yes, thank you so much for noticing Milo. How did you see him?"

She gave a small shrug. "I was keeping an eye on all the kids."

While managing to hold a conversation with me? I couldn't keep my thoughts off how beautiful she was, yet she managed to watch all the kids playing and answer my questions. Was this woman a superhuman?

"Well, thank you. I'm so grateful you got to him before something bad happened."

She smiled and looked at Milo. "We're all good now, right?"

He sniffed and nodded before giving her a hug. It only lasted a few seconds before he took off running with Finn at his side.

She stood and brushed off her hands while I remained frozen in place. Milo hugged her. He hadn't hugged anyone since Olivia left. Not me, not any of the women from the Pride, not even Finn.

"Is everything okay?" Her concerned expression pulled me out of my shock.

"Yes, it's great. If you want the job it's yours."

Her eyebrows shot up. "Really? Don't you want to ask me more questions?"

"I don't think I need to."

She let out a breath and beamed. "I think we should discuss the specifics, but I'd really love the opportunity."

We headed back to the bench while the boys went to a sandy area to play. "Chloe said you committed to a year. I'd really like someone to stay until they finish kindergarten."

She pursed her lips. "So next May?"

I nodded.

"Fourteen months," she muttered under her breath.

"Is that a problem?" I didn't think it would be that big of a problem, but it seemed like those two added months might be a deal breaker.

She shook her head. "No, that's okay."

"I know you're new to the area. Are you locked into a contract for an apartment?"

"No, not yet. I was waiting until I found a job so I would know what area to look in," she replied.

"Well, I was hoping whoever took the job would be willing to move in."

Her back straightened. I wanted to shake myself. Asking a stranger to move in with me wasn't my best move.

"Into the pool house," I quickly clarified. "It has its own kitchen and bathroom and a decent sized bedroom."

That seemed to help her relax a bit. "That would be great."

"Oh good." Now for the most awkward part. Money. "My schedule isn't very normal or consistent. I can't make hours like nine to five work."

She seemed a bit confused.

"I can usually get up with the boys and take them to preschool. It's the afternoon and evening that I really need help with."

"Oh right. That's fine."

"And some weekends," I added.

She nodded. "Okay."

"And I travel quite a bit." I wasn't sure how much Chloe explained. Hopefully, this wasn't too much to ask. "I've been having the boys stay with Emma or one of the others while I'm gone, but I'd really like for you to stay with the boys."

She didn't hesitate. "Brandon, I don't have anything else going on in my life right now. I know that makes me sound kind of pathetic, but this job will be my entire world. Whatever you need, I can make work."

Did that mean she didn't have a boyfriend?

No. Stop it. She had the time and attention to give to my boys. That was what mattered. And I wasn't interested in a relationship. I couldn't balance everything going on as it was. Adding in dating was the furthest thing from what I needed in my life.

"Are you sure?"

She smiled. "Yes, I can handle your crazy schedule. I don't need time off, and I'll even stay here through the holidays. I can give one hundred percent to the boys."

There was no way she was this perfect. Chloe and I spent a half-hour discussing the salary I should offer, but suddenly I wanted to double it.

"So, you're okay with crazy hours, being on call, possibly even traveling with them?"

"Yes, Brandon," she said with confidence.

"The salary I'm offering is fifteen hundred a week. It works out to be seventy-eight thousand a year." I hated this part. Money was such an awkward topic, but I needed to get it out now. I was asking so much of her. She was basically giving up fourteen months of her life for my family. I wanted to pay her a lot more, but Chloe kept me from handing over all my paychecks.

She didn't flinch. "Yes, that's fine."

That was a relief. Hopefully, we never had to discuss it again. "Wonderful. Can you start tomorrow?"

"Of course," she said with enthusiasm.

I smiled. "If you can come over at nine, I'll give you a run-through and you can get settled in before having to pick up the boys."

"That sounds great."

I called the boys over to officially introduce them. "Milo, Finn, this is Sydney. She's going to be staying with us and picking you up from school from now on."

Finn cocked his head. "Are you going to play with us?"

Sydney giggled. "Yes, we can play every day."

"Can you make grilled cheese?" Milo asked.

"I can," she confirmed.

That seemed to be all the boys needed to know. They smiled and turned to me.

"Sounds good?" I looked at each of them.

"Yeah!" They cheered before running back to play.

"I guess they're sold," I said with a laugh. I shouldn't have been surprised they were so easily won over. Sydney had me from the moment I saw her too.

4

SYDNEY

I double-checked the address then stared up at the house. Mansion?

This was the right place. I guess the whole pool house, one-bedroom apartment should have been a warning, but it wasn't. It didn't click in my naive brain that when someone had a pool house that usually meant the main home was gigantic.

My eighteen-year-old Civic stuck out in this beautiful neighborhood. It seemed like everything had been hand-picked and coordinated along each street. Brandon lived at the top of a long hill overlooking the entire Salt Lake Valley. I was right about him being a fancy pants. I just didn't think it would affect me like this. I wasn't normally one to feel self-conscious. Life was too short to compare yourself to others, but this... this was wealth I'd only seen from afar. Or on TV.

I took in a calming breath and got out. He hired me based on my experiences, references, and interactions. He met me and liked me well enough to offer me the job. That was enough.

Not like I would have turned him down. Especially not when he told me the pay. Almost eighty grand! In a year?

That was more than I'd made in the last ten years combined. As overwhelming as the idea of staying here for fourteen months was, I could do anything for that kind of money. It would be more than enough to set myself up in another country. Anywhere in the world I wanted.

I got to the massive wooden door and knocked. A moment later it swung open and two adorable smiling faces peered up at me.

"Sydney!" Milo ran forward and wrapped his arms around my legs.

I rubbed his back. "Hi Milo."

Finn stood back, watching me with curious eyes.

"Hi Finn."

He cocked his head. "You know I'm Finn?"

I nodded. They were identical twins, but I noticed Milo's hair was cut a bit shorter yesterday and that Finn was the more observant one. While Milo was the leader and took off looking for their next thrill, Finn was a few steps behind taking it all in.

I grinned while he seemed to consider this.

"Sometimes Mommy can't tell," he replied.

That was the first time anyone had mentioned their mother. I'd wondered where she was and if she had a say in who filled the nanny position, but Brandon mentioned he was a single parent. What happened to her?

I followed them through the entryway, taking in all the details of the beautiful home. The dark wood floors paired perfectly with the cool gray walls. Just after the entry, the room opened up to reveal a huge open staircase going both upstairs and down to a basement. There was an office past the stairs, and I noticed a bunch of sports memorabilia decorating its walls and shelves. Brandon must be a fan.

The boys led me farther into the house until we reached the most beautiful kitchen I'd ever seen. It was massive. Floor to ceiling cabinets along two walls, top of the line appliances, and an enormous island with five bar stools covered in ivory leather. Every inch screamed luxury.

Brandon was standing in front of the stove and turned as we entered. I spotted scrambled eggs in the pan and tried not to cringe at the slight smell of something burning. "Good morning, Sydney. Sorry I didn't hear the door."

"We heard, Daddy," Finn said as he used all his strength to pull himself up on a stool.

"Good job. Thanks for being a helper." Brandon smiled at his son before turning back around.

I continued to look around the room and wandered to the closest doorway. It revealed a formal dining room. The walls were gray with intricate wainscoting and a giant crystal chandelier hung over the twelve-person table.

I was trying really hard to not get overwhelmed, but I literally just walked into how the other half lives. My last apartment in Denver could have fit in the dining room. I hadn't even seen the living rooms or bedrooms yet.

"Milo, Finn, do you want to give Sydney a tour?" Brandon's voice pulled me back into the kitchen.

"Yeah!" They ran to me and each took a hand before pulling me back to the stairs. I saw their bedroom, which was jungle themed complete with a mural of animals and greenery that covered two walls. Their beds were built to look like they were a part of the tree canopy. It was over the top and amazing. They showed me their slide and bridges that took them to different play areas built on platforms.

"This is so cool. Do you guys love your room?"

They nodded in unison before running down the hall, pointing out their race car themed playroom which looked like a toy store exploded, a guest room, and their dad's room.

They took me down to the basement where another guest room and theater room were located. There was more down there, but they didn't seem to care to show me everything, just their favorite places. Back on the main floor, they pointed out their dad's office and I got a quick look in. I didn't notice before, but all the memorabilia was hockey related. I guessed that was Brandon's favorite sport.

"Come on, Sydney." Finn pulled my hand to follow him through the stunning yet cozy living room to the wall of glass doors that overlooked the backyard. There was a pool with a rock formation that created two slides and a playset that nearly put the one yesterday to shame. It was three stories tall with a zip line, rock wall, and at least five slides. Why would they ever want to leave their house when they had all of this at their fingertips?

Nannying with this much to entertain them was going to be a cinch.

"Boys, come eat," Brandon called from the door that led to the kitchen several yards from me. I headed toward him as the boys came running in.

He had eggs and dark, nearly black, toast ready for them at the island and they quickly claimed their seats and dug in. While they were eating, Brandon moved toward me.

"Like I said yesterday, most mornings I can take them to preschool unless I'm out of town or we have an early game so I have to be to the arena early."

I nodded then paused. "The arena?"

He eyed me before turning to the boys. "Hey, less talking and more eating. We can't be late today." When they were focused, he returned to me. "Yeah, that's where practices are as well as games."

I quickly ran through everything the women told me about him. Not much. He had a bunch of hockey stuff, maybe he was an agent. I looked around the kitchen and panicked. Was he the team owner? This guy was obviously wealthy, but I didn't realize it was like *own a team* crazy money.

"Right." I was too embarrassed to ask what he did. I should have probably covered that at the park. I'd figure it out eventually. Maybe the boys would clue me in later.

"You can bring the boys to practices if you want. Chloe, Emma, and Kendall are usually there with the rest of the women from the Pride."

"The Pride?" I asked, clearing missing something.

"Yeah the wives and girlfriends. They're really nice. I'm sure you'll get along with them."

What on earth? The wives and girlfriends of who? And what practice? I couldn't wait. I had to know.

"Brandon," I interrupted. "I'm confused. What exactly do you do?"

He raised an eyebrow. "Did they not tell you my position?"

I shook my head, relieved he understood.

"I'm a center."

I blinked at him wondering if I'd misheard. Was that corporate lingo I didn't know?

"A center?" I hated how dumb I was sounding, but I was getting more stumped by the second.

"Yeah, on the offense."

Center. Offense. Those were sports words. I nodded along like I finally got it.

"Daddy's the best center in the league," Milo said with a proud grin.

"I think Hartman might argue that," Brandon teased back. I smiled like I was in on the joke. *Hartman? Who was that?*

"Can we go to the game?" Finn asked. "You promised we could go to a game this week."

Milo watched his brother before joining in and nodding in sync.

"Not tonight, let's give Sydney a chance to settle in. How about Monday?" Brandon sighed and looked at me. "Would you mind? I did promise them if they were good they could come."

As if I had a clue what I was agreeing to I smiled. "Sure."

His shoulders relaxed. "Thanks. I'll have the front office reserve tickets for you guys."

He wasn't going to be there with us? Where would he be?

"Sydney, do you have a jersey?" Milo asked.

"No, I don't." I still wasn't positive about what sport or team we were going to be watching, but I did know that there wasn't a single jersey or sports themed shirt in my possession.

"You have an extra one, right?" Finn looked to his dad.

Brandon nodded. "I'll make sure she has one."

"You have to wear Daddy's number with us, so people know who we're cheering for," Milo said as he bounced in his seat.

M y head spun as all the pieces fell into place. Brandon was wealthy, had a crazy schedule, went to practice every day, worked at the arena. He was a center, on offense.

I stared at him while he washed off the boys' now empty plates.

The hockey stuff in the office. It was his. Like *his.*

I was a nanny for a professional athlete. For a player in the NHL. "Oh."

Brandon eyed me. "Oh, what?"

I wasn't normally easily impressed by money or fame. When I lived in LA and ran into a singer or actor, I didn't care much.

This was different. I admired athletes. Probably because sports were the only thing my dad got excited about, and if I wanted anything to talk about with him it was usually related to who was looking good this year or what team should make it to playoffs. I didn't know very much about hockey, Dad's more of a baseball guy, but I learned enough to know that if they made it to the professional level, they had dedicated their entire lives to one thing. They pushed their bodies to the limit. They left it all on the line. They were focused and driven. They were everything I wasn't.

"I didn't realize you were a hockey player."

It shouldn't have changed anything, knowing who he was, but it did. I respected him. I was proud of him, and I hadn't even seen him play yet. I pulled myself together before he noticed I was fangirling over him.

His smile wavered. "Chloe and Emma didn't mention that?"

I shook my head. "It never came up."

This didn't change anything. I was still watching over Milo and Finn, living in the pool house, and Brandon was my boss. He chose me. He interviewed me and decided I was good enough. That was what mattered. He trusted me to care for his boys. It was the highest compliment anyone could give me. I had to work hard and do everything in my power to show him I was worthy of his trust. What he did for a living didn't matter.

I suddenly noticed how tight his shirt was around his biceps as he crossed his arms across his wide chest. Had his shoulders been that thick and broad yesterday at the park? How did I miss that?

Because I wasn't checking out my potential boss. Like I definitely was now.

Of course, his job, and especially his body, shouldn't change my view of him. I couldn't get all flustered now. I most definitely couldn't find my boss attractive. That was the very last thing I needed.

"Huh." He smirked. "I guess I should have mentioned that sooner. I just assume people know."

I shrugged. Admitting I didn't watch hockey didn't seem like the right thing to tell a professional player.

"I'm a centerman for the Utah Fury."

"I put that together," I said with my own smirk which

made him laugh. It was a lovely sound. I couldn't help but notice the way he relaxed and how his shoulders bounced. He wasn't the uptight businessman I expected. Nope, this was much worse.

He was off-limits. I needed this job too much to get distracted. Heaven knows I'd somehow made it awkward, and I needed to survive fourteen months. Plus, it wasn't like he would ever see me like that. He was a freaking hockey player. I was a transient cursed with a wanderlust so strong I couldn't stay put for longer than a few months. He was at the peak of his career and my resume was full of minimum wage jobs. I'd never cared, until now. I was proud of not being tied down, free to go where my heart took me.

It was hard not to compare myself to women like Chloe and Emma. They seemed so happy, established, mature.

"So I noticed you move around a lot."

I bit my lip and nodded. "I like to travel and see new places."

"I bet you have some good stories."

"A few."

"Is that why you hesitated when I asked for you to stay for a few extra months?" He asked.

"Kind of. I have a dream of traveling around the world. I want to see all seven continents. I want to live in different countries, immerse myself in different cultures. I want to understand people. I want to know them and love them."

"That's beautiful." He stared at me and I had to fight not to fidget.

"Most people think it's crazy."

"I don't. I think it's amazing."

Those words meant so much. I wasn't used to people understanding when I explained my dreams. It certainly didn't help diminish my attraction to him.

I was twenty-eight and still searching for myself. Chasing every whim like a leaf on the wind. I'd never regret my choices. Each experience added something to me. They built me into the woman I was, and Brandon thought that was enough. Well, enough for his boys. I was silly to wonder if that meant I was enough for him. Nothing could happen between us. He was my boss. The one who wrote the checks that ensured my freedom and funded my next great adventure. I was here to save up and finally live out my dreams. Forming any attachments was pointless; I'd be gone at the end of the contract.

5

BRANDON

"You're telling me she didn't know who you were?" Hartman asked with a chuckle.

"I knew I shouldn't have told you guys." I ignored him and moved to the squat rack. I mentioned Sydney's confusion during practice and they weren't letting it go. The topic had somehow followed us into the weight room, gaining even more attention. I wanted them to drop it, but I knew better. The more you protested, the more the guys clung to a topic.

"Must have been humbling," Erik teased. "When was the last time that happened?"

I looked to the ceiling while lifting the bar onto my shoulders and rolling it down a few inches before squatting. I focused on my form and breathing while the rest of them laughed at my expense.

"She's not from here," Reese said diplomatically. "Just because all the women we know eat, sleep, and breathe hockey doesn't mean that's normal."

Nikolai grunted. "That's good she didn't know."

The rest of the guys turned to the quiet Russian. If he chose to say something it was usually worth listening to. I finished my set and grabbed my water bottle while I waited for him to continue.

"She didn't take the job because of who you are or what you do."

I nodded. "Yeah, she had no idea what I was going to offer to pay her either. She saved Milo from a broken arm or leg before I told her anything. That's what made me hire her."

"Not her long legs or perfect smile?" Olli asked as he passed me for his turn to squat.

I narrowed my eyes at him while the rest of the guys seemed to move closer.

He shrugged. "What? Emma's words not mine."

"Wait, she's hot too?" Jason, one of the younger guys on the team, jumped into the conversation.

This was the first time in a long time that so many guys were interested in my life. I mostly kept to myself, not sharing my personal drama with the team. I was closest to Olli and Hartman, but being one of the oldest guys on the team, and having the oldest children, set me apart. I didn't go out with them after games or discuss girl problems with the younger guys. Up until recently, I was the boring married guy. I even earned the nickname 'Dad.'

"She's attractive, yes." I felt uncomfortable talking about my sons' nanny like this, but I'd have to be blind to not recognize that Sydney was a beautiful woman. Also, a very off-limits woman.

"Dad's blushing!" Eric called loud enough to gain the attention of everyone in the weight room.

I shot him a glare and turned to Olli. "Hurry up."

He smirked and did one more deep squat before replacing the bar and moving out of my way. This was why I didn't spend much time with the guys on the team. They were like school girls sometimes. Thriving off gossip and drama. Plus, they were relentless with their teasing. The best thing I could do was not react. Like I did with Milo and Finn when they were acting up.

I smiled to myself. I was either with *this* roomful of little kids or at home with mine.

"You do know what this means, right?" Reese bumped shoulders with Erik while they watched me with devious smiles.

"What's that?" Erik encouraged his brother-in-law.

"Dad's next," Reese replied.

I ignored the ominous statement and blocked them out. Well, I tried to.

"You know, if you had said that last week, I never would have believed you," Olli joined in. "Things with Olivia were so terrible I didn't think he would ever look at another woman without getting nauseous, but look at him now. Blushing over the nanny. I think you might be onto something."

Reese's grin grew. "It's always the ones we least expect."

"Yeah, we learned that lesson when Mr. Russia grew a heart and Derek found someone to tolerate him," Erik said with a growing smirk.

"Hey!" Derek shouted from the free weight area across the room.

I glanced at Nikolai for his reaction, but he just grunted and mumbled something. Probably in Russian.

"What?" Erik chuckled. "You all know it's true."

Hartman agreed along with the rest of the guys listening to the conversation, which was just about everyone.

Amelia, Derek's girlfriend and Nikolai's sister-in-law, walked into the room. She was recently brought on as the team trainer, though she usually stayed out of sight in the training room.

"What's going on in here?" She looked around like she was ready to discipline a class of first graders.

"Dad's got a crush!" Derek shouted helpfully from the other side of the room.

Her brows pulled together and she searched until her eyes landed on me. "Really?" Her voice was much quieter now and she made her way over. Perfect. As soon as she left the room the entire Pride would be notified.

"No, not really. They're making things up," I rushed out before any of the guys could speak.

"He said she's attractive," Erik inserted.

She narrowed her eyes. "Who is?"

"His nanny," Reese answered.

She shot the guys a glare. "Can you let him speak for himself?"

Yeah, that wasn't likely to happen.

She spun to face me. "You found a nanny?"

It was a bit surprising she hadn't already heard through the grapevine, but maybe it wasn't an interesting enough piece of news to make the rounds. Until now.

I should have kept my mouth shut.

"Yes. Actually, Kendall, Chloe, and Emma found her. She started today," I answered.

Her face softened. "That's really great, Brandon. I hope she helps take some of the burden off your shoulders."

I nodded. "I think she will."

She moved a half step closer and lowered her voice. "If you ever need help, please let me know. I know our schedules are pretty much the same, but I have more flexibility than you."

"Thanks, but with Sydney around I should be okay."

She smiled. "Good. I hope I can meet her soon."

"She's bringing the boys to the game next week."

"Then I'll track her down," she said with a nod.

"I'm sure she'll appreciate being welcomed in."

Amelia seemed satisfied and went back to her office.

"She's coming to a game?" Hartman asked while wagging his brows. "You already trying to impress her?"

I closed my eyes and counted to three like I did when the twins were driving me crazy. "The boys asked to come. She's coming by default."

"Oh right, because she didn't even know you were on the team," Erik pointed out again and started a new round of laughter.

This was the last time I told them anything. Ever again.

I hoped as more of them got married and started their families they would mature and maybe even mellow out. I was wrong. It was bad enough to deal with the prying of the women, but the guys were usually worse.

"That means we'll get to meet her," Olli pointed out, making my stomach drop.

"None of you will say anything to her about this conversation." I gave them my best stern dad look.

A few of them dipped their heads, but Erik and Olli seemed to take it as a challenge.

"Don't worry, Dad. We won't embarrass you," Erik said not sounding one bit genuine.

"Yeah, we'll be on our best behavior." Olli winked.

"We don't want another Olivia situation," Erik said with a dramatic shudder.

"What's that supposed to mean?" I asked.

"We don't want her, or anyone taking advantage of you." He sighed. "That's why I'm honestly glad she didn't know who you were."

Olli nodded. "She's in a really unique position, one she could manipulate or abuse. Emma and Chloe said her references were great, but that doesn't mean any of us are letting our guards down."

Erik agreed. "We'll be nice, but we want you to be smart. Don't get distracted by her good looks."

"I mean, she's probably safe since she didn't even know who you were." Olli teased.

"What is it, thirty years in the NHL and still no one knows who he is," Erik chuckled.

I shook my head and walked away from them. They could joke all they wanted, but the moment I realized she'd had no idea who I was would go down as one of the best in my life. She didn't know who the women were when she talked to them in the café. She didn't know I was anyone other than a single dad needing help. When we met at the park, she didn't see what car I drove, where I lived, or had any idea how much money I had.

She was interested in the job before any of that could influence her. She didn't care about my status or fame. She was the complete opposite of my ex. I didn't think it was possible to meet someone and just be me anymore. It was refreshing. It helped me trust her even more.

I didn't know her story or much about her at all, but I could tell by her actions she was a good, genuine person. That was all that mattered to me.

It was after six when I got home. I wasn't sure what I was going to walk into. Part of me didn't want to find out. What if the boys went wild? What if they drove her crazy and she was waiting for me to come in so she could leave? What if she decided this wasn't what she wanted after all? The boys were generally pretty good. I didn't hear many complaints from their preschool, but when they were home they liked to run around and weren't necessarily on their best behavior. Some days it was too much for me, and they were my kids. I loved them unconditionally. Sydney didn't have that built in.

There was only one way to find out.

I hit the button to open the garage and parked. The boys didn't come running out, so that was a good sign. Maybe. They could also be locked in their room because Sydney couldn't handle them.

With a deep breath, I opened the door and walked through the mudroom, dropping my duffle on the bench. I listened for any sign of where they were, and followed the sound of laughter upstairs. I checked their bedroom but it was empty, so I moved on to their playroom and peeked in. All three of them were on the ground racing cars along a course outlined in blue tape. There was a paper sign at the beginning that said 'Cullen Race Track' with hand-drawn checkered flags below. It was an impressive course with curves and turns that overlapped the design. It took up most of the floor. They must have been working on it since they got home from school.

She leaned back on her heels and pulled out her phone. I watched her take a few photos and the familiar anger worked its way from my stomach.

"Hey guys." I stepped into the room and their laughter quieted.

"Daddy!" Finn jumped up and gave me a hug.

Milo stayed in his spot but smiled and waved. "Look what Sydney made for us!"

I forced a smile. "It's pretty amazing."

"I've won twice, and Milo won one time. Sydney hasn't won at all," Finn said with a giggle. "She's not as good at cars as we are."

I glanced at her and she pursed her lips, making a funny face at the boys. "You guys have had a lot more practice. Once my body gets used to crawling on the ground, you better watch out."

Milo giggled like she just said the funniest thing he'd ever heard.

She shook her head and looked up at me. "How was practice?"

"Fine. Would you mind talking out here?" I moved into the hall and listened to make sure the boys continued playing.

Sydney leaned against the wall opposite me and smiled. "What's up?"

"Were you just taking pictures of the boys?"

She flinched. "Oh, yeah."

I clenched my jaw but forced myself to relax. She wasn't Olivia. This wasn't the same.

"I would prefer that you don't take pictures of the boys."

She stared at me for a second. "Okay. I just wasn't sure if they would still be interested by the time you got home, so I wanted to get some action shots to show you of them playing."

That wasn't what I was expecting.

"They're for me?"

She nodded, looking confused. "Who else would I show?"

"Your followers?" I said with a shrug.

"My followers?" She asked.

"On social media."

She laughed. She actually laughed at me. "Brandon, I don't have any social media accounts."

"You don't?" I didn't quite believe her.

"No, I found myself checking them too much. I didn't like that I compared myself to what I saw. I realized they weren't adding anything to my life, besides anxiety, so I deleted everything... five or six years ago."

I blinked. She was the complete opposite of everything Olivia was. In the most perfect way.

"I'm sorry. I appreciate you taking pictures to show me. I..." I paused and rubbed my jaw. "My ex was obsessed with her social media. She moved to California in order to grow her career as an influencer or model or whatever she called herself. It left a bit of a bad taste for me."

Her eyes widened. "I'm so sorry. I had no idea. I swear the pictures I take are only for you and me."

I relaxed my shoulders. "Thank you."

She smiled and touched my arm as she passed me to go back into the playroom. I tried not to watch her, but I was like a moth to a flame. I needed to forget what the guys said in the weight room. There was no crush or attraction to Sydney. She was the boys' nanny. That's it.

I figured if I told myself that a hundred or so times, I might actually start believing it. Could take a month or so, but I'd get there.

"Oh, I wasn't sure when you would be back so the boys already ate."

Right. The kids. That was why she was here. Focus.

"Thanks, that's great. I'll let you know if there are days when I'll be home in time to eat with them."

"Daddy, she *can* make grilled cheese. They're good," Milo confirmed and Sydney looked proud.

"I'm glad I got your approval," she said with a laugh.

"He's a tough critic. It took me a few attempts to get it right, so you're lucky you got it on your first try."

She looked at the boys. "It's all about the perfect amount of gooey cheese, huh?"

They nodded. "Yeah!"

It was amazing how comfortable they were around her. I thought they would be more hesitant, especially since they hadn't had a stranger in their life for a while. I was just grateful Olivia didn't manage to harden their warm hearts. They were probably starving for a feminine influence.

"I'm going to grab something to eat." I wasn't sure what to do. I was home now, but the boys were more than content playing with her. Did she want to leave? Was she done for the day? I probably should have figured this out before right now.

"Okay, we have a race to finish and then we can head down and have the dessert we made, right?" she addressed the boys and they quickly agreed.

"Sounds good." I backed out of the room, grateful she had a plan. This was a whole new world for both of us. I had some research to do on what to expect from her and how to make sure we were on the same page.

I opened the fridge and freezer, searching for something to eat. There was a container of something pink in the freezer, so I pulled it out and lifted the lid. It looked like sorbet or ice cream. After a sniff test I was pretty sure it was strawberry. This must be the dessert they made. I put it back and pulled out the grilled chicken and rice I usually ate.

She was here for the boys, but I couldn't help but get excited about the surprises I was sure to find daily. Not only were the boys alive and fed, they were laughing and having fun. No tears or begging for me. They didn't even seem to care I was home.

She was nothing like Olivia. She was here for the right reasons. I wasn't going to let the guys get in my head.

6

SYDNEY

The pool house was nicer than my parents' home in Pennsylvania. It was far nicer than any hotel I'd stayed at. It was decorated in gray and white, much like the main house, giving it a warm, inviting feel. The bedroom had a queen bed, walk-in closet, and dresser so there was plenty of room for me to put away my meager possessions. I hadn't expected to feel comfortable living in someone else's home, but the boys and Brandon never came near, so I was able to quickly get used to it being my space after a day or two. On Saturday, I spent the afternoon with the boys while Brandon had practice, and on Sunday he spent the whole day with them. I had a chance to explore more of the city and familiarize myself with the area. By Monday, I was getting used to the routine.

The boys were already gone when I walked into the main house—I still couldn't believe that was something in my vocabulary now—to see what I could make them as a snack after I picked them up from preschool.

A black and maroon jersey with *Cullen* written out across the top was waiting for me on the island. I picked it up and couldn't help but grin. Not only was I going to my first hockey game tonight, but I was also wearing one of the player's jerseys. His personal jersey! Never in my wildest dreams did I think something like that would happen.

Part of me wanted to call and tell my dad, but he'd stopped answering my calls two years ago when I told them I wasn't coming home for Christmas. I'd been living in Seattle and couldn't afford the trip. When Dad offered to pay for my ticket, I turned him down. Not because I didn't want to come, but because I knew spending that type of money would be hard for them, too. I couldn't say that though, not without offending them. They were offended anyway, so much so that they told me not to bother calling or coming home ever again.

Mom emailed me once to let me know my last living grandparent, my dad's mom, passed away. Again, I couldn't afford to attend the funeral, but she hadn't even invited me. I replied but never heard back from her.

Dad might like to go to a game. I could ask Brandon about getting tickets for when they played the Philadelphia team, but then again, that would require my parents to drive two hours. That was as likely to happen as them forgiving me.

I set the jersey back down and pushed them out of my mind. They chose to live their lives in a tiny bubble. I couldn't control that. If they were happy then I had to leave them be.

The fridge was well-stocked. I found out Brandon's assistant did the grocery shopping, so I didn't even have to worry about that. My only responsibility was caring for the boys and keeping them happy, which wasn't that hard. They were so good and so desperate for attention that simply playing with them made them completely content.

Neither of them had mentioned their mother or missing her. I wanted to know what the story was but it wasn't my place or my business. I had a suspicion that I could find out online— there had to be information about his ex— but I felt like if Brandon wanted me to know he would tell me himself.

I pulled out some fruit and cut it up before putting it in baggies so the boys could munch on it in the car on the way home. I swear, after a few hours of playing with their classmates, they were as ravenous as if they'd been starved for days.

The drive to their school was short but I basked in the silence, knowing it was about to end for the day. I parked and went into the waiting area just past the doors. The school preferred that parents wait for the children to come out rather than interrupting the other classes. I wasn't sure how my appearance could disrupt a bunch of three- to five-year olds' playing, but I followed the rules.

The woman at the front smiled. "Good afternoon, Miss Sydney. I'll go get the boys for you."

"Thanks." Brandon had notified the school that I'd be picking the boys up, so when I showed up Friday, they were prepared. I'd been worried they wouldn't let me take the boys home, but once I showed my ID and they took my picture for their system I was all set.

"Sydney!" Milo and Finn ran toward me and barreled into my legs, wrapping their arms around me.

"Hi boys." I rubbed their backs for a second before stepping away. "Are you guys ready?"

They nodded and we went back to the car. They were pretty good at buckling themselves in, so I just had to double-check while they dug into the snacks they found waiting for them.

"I love strawberries so much," Finn said with a content smile.

He'd loved the sorbet we made using his favorite fruit, so I made a mental note to make sure we always had them on hand. Getting the boys to eat healthy was challenging enough. They were used to fast food kids' meals, but I

47

wanted to wean them off that as quickly as possible. Discovering one of his top choices so quickly was like striking gold.

Milo willingly ate the strawberries in his bag, but he'd told me yesterday that watermelon was his top favorite. As soon as they were in season, I promised I'd buy him the biggest one we could find.

Once they were situated and I climbed in, I turned to face them. "What do you guys want to do today? Park, home, or museum."

Brandon gave me their family pass to the children's museum last night in case they ever wanted to go. It was closer than the zoo, and since it was indoors, it was a much better option for the hot Utah summers. I had a feeling we'd be there quite a bit over the next few months.

"Can we go to the wood park?" Milo asked.

Wood park? I only knew of the park I met them at, but that one was metal and sand. No wood anywhere.

"Yeah, the big wood one." Finn cheered.

Good. They were locked in on that one. I knew better than to try talking them out of something. A couple of days with them and I'd learned that was like negotiating with the very best lawyer. Not going to work out in my favor.

They continued eating and talking to each other about this amazing park while I did a quick search on my phone. *Wood park in Salt Lake City* brought up nothing. Of course not. I needed a bit more information, but it wasn't like the four-year-olds had an address.

The only phone numbers I had for people here were Brandon and Chloe. Brandon had practice, and I doubted Chloe had any idea either, but she was my only option.

I called her and waited.

"Sydney, is everything okay?" Her voice didn't sound anxious, just a bit surprised.

"Yes, sorry. The boys are fine. They just asked me to take

48

them to the big wood park and I have no idea where that is. I tried searching for it online, but nothing came up."

She let out a single laugh. "I'm not the park expert either, but let me see if anyone in the office knows."

I waited as I heard her call out if anyone knew of the wood park in the area. The responses were mumbled but I wasn't holding out much hope.

"Ask them if the playground looks like a castle," she finally said to me.

I peeked at the boys through the rearview mirror. "Does the wood park look like a castle?"

Finn nodded aggressively while Milo beamed. "Yeah! There's a flag with a dragon and a drawbridge."

I relayed the information to Chloe who passed it along to someone on her end.

"Okay, yeah that's the one. It's up on the bench. It's actually pretty close to my house." She paused. "Huh, good to know. Emma probably knows where it is. Anyway, I'll send you the location so you can follow the directions on your phone."

"Thank you so much!" I couldn't believe we figured it out together.

"No problem. I'll send you Emma's number too so if you get lost, she can help you."

"Perfect. I appreciate it."

"I'll see you guys tonight at the game, right?"

"Yeah, we'll be there." I glanced back at the boys.

"Okay, see you later."

She hung up and within seconds I got a text with the address. I got the directions and soon we were on our way.

"All right, boys. Wood park here we come!"

They cheered like I just told them tomorrow was Christmas. It amazed me how easy it was to make them happy. Hopefully this wasn't just a honeymoon phase.

We got there without issue, and sure enough, the park

had an enormous wooden castle with slides, swings, rock walls, and horses you could rock on. Its real name was Rockwell Park, but Wood Park clearly made more sense. The boys took off across the drawbridge and I lost sight of them as they climbed but a few moments later their blond heads reappeared at the very top near the dragon flag. They waved down to me and I returned the gesture while pulling on my sunglasses.

As tough as it must have been to have two newborns, then toddlers, it was nice that they had each other to play with. I reaped the benefits for sure. They were content chasing each other, rather than showing off for me. I decided the number one word used at any park was "watch." Every three seconds some child shouted it.

The boys got my attention a few times, but for the most part they played well with each other. I made sure to keep them within sight at all times, moving along the sidewalk that created the border. Most of the adults were either on their phones or chatting on the benches, but I felt wrong doing either of those things. I was here to care for the boys. I'd been able to catch Milo before he fell last time, and I hoped to prevent either of them from getting hurt. I couldn't do that if I was staring at my phone.

I meandered around, watching all the activity. Younger children screaming, a woman attempting to feed a baby while also chastising her toddler for pushing another child, a man talking on the phone with his back to the playground.

People watching was one of my favorite activities, and with the boys I had a feeling I was going to be doing it a lot. I never wanted to judge anyone, especially when I was only getting a tiny glimpse into their lives, but it was fun to make up stories about who they were.

I wondered what people thought about me? Did they think I was a hippie, like some people had called me in the past? I liked loud patterns and flowy clothes. I didn't think that was all that strange. Plus, my loose pants made it easy to get on the ground and play with the boys or climb behind them at the park.

"Sydney! Look up here!" Finn called down from the top of the tallest slide. Of course, that's where they were.

"Hey!" I waved, and they jumped together, flying down the slick metal.

"They're yours?" The woman next to me took a step closer.

I wasn't sure how to reply. Did she mean like mine, biologically? Mine to watch? The ones I was here with? I just smiled and nodded.

"They're cute. You're so lucky to have twins. They can entertain themselves for you." She pointed at a little girl making her way across a swaying bridge. "I told her she has to play on her own for five minutes so I could have a break."

I chuckled. "Yeah it's nice they have an automatic best friend."

"How old are they?" she asked.

"Four." I wasn't sure where this conversation was going. Maybe this was normal? Adults chatting with strangers while their kids played. That seemed to make sense. I didn't usually struggle this much with small talk, but the park and children were new territory for me. I didn't know the customs yet.

Milo and Finn were climbing back to the top of the slide, and I noticed her little girl wasn't far behind. Did she want me to get them to play together? Was that what we did at the park? There wasn't exactly an instruction manual for playground etiquette.

"So is Alice," she said with a smile.

Okay then. I nodded and took a few steps out on the wood chips that covered the play area and shouted to the boys. "Milo, Finn, come down here for a second."

They raced each other to the slide, Milo getting down first but closely followed by Finn. They stopped in front of me with bright red faces. If they didn't slow down soon, they were going to be out of energy before the game started tonight. Were they too old to take a nap? Another thing to look into.

"See that girl?" I lowered to their level and pointed to the cute little brunette with bright pink leggings on. They nodded in sync. "Her name is Alice and she doesn't have a friend here to play with. Do you think you guys could be her friend and invite her to play?"

I waited, not sure how they would react. Finn spun to face me with a wide smile. "Okay!"

Milo took off running. "Alice! Want to be our friend?" His shouts drew the attention of everyone at the park, but he didn't care.

The little girl stopped and stared down at them for a moment before smiling. "Yes."

I watched until the three of them met and started running together before returning to the sidewalk.

The woman was beaming. "Thank you so much. I really appreciate you getting them to include her. She's so shy. She won't ever be the first to ask to play with anyone, but if someone comes to her, she'll open up."

"No problem." The boys seemed to be having fun with their new addition, so I shrugged. Call me the kid matchmaker.

"I'm Melanie." She offered her hand.

I shook it, feeling a bit awkward. This was too formal for a playground. "Sydney."

"Do you guys come to this park often?"

I smiled to myself at the twist on the overused pick up line. "This is my first time with them here, but they really like it. We'll probably come once a week or so."

She seemed curious.

"I'm their new nanny."

Her eyes widened. "Wow. Really? You seem so comfortable with them."

"They're pretty awesome, so it's easy."

"I never would have guessed." She smiled at me and I turned back to the kids. Was it really that strange that the boys and I were already bonding? It felt natural being with them. Like my little buddies and this job were meant for me.

A few minutes later, I heard yelling and scanned the playground for the source. Milo was standing at the top of a ladder blocking Finn and Alice from reaching the top. He was the one yelling.

I hurried over. "Milo, what's going on?"

His angry eyes found mine and he hit his fists against his sides. "Finn said he's king and Alice is queen and I can't play with them."

I turned to Finn. "Did you say that?"

He hung onto the ladder and didn't meet my eyes.

"Finn, you guys need to play nice with each other."

"But he said there can be two kings. I don't want two kings. He can be a horse." Finn said through a pout.

Melanie reached my side and looked between the kids. "Alice, are you being nice?"

The little girl's cheeks reddened.

I was so far out of my element. I wasn't an expert of playground etiquette or how to navigate feuds. The boys were always so great together. I felt horrible for a moment when I blamed the new addition, but it wasn't Alice's fault. They needed to learn how to get along with new people.

"I don't want to be a horse!" Milo screamed.

"Then don't play with us!" Finn's volume matched his brother.

Crap. This was getting out of hand. I needed to come up with a plan. "Um. Milo, how about you be a very special knight."

I tried that, thinking it was best to stay within the game

they started. His eyes flickered to mine and I continued. "You could be on a mission to make sure the path is safe for the king and queen."

I checked on Finn and he was listening intently.

"Milo will pick which direction you should go then he'll tell you if it's safe or…" My mind went blank.

"He might have to fight a dragon." Melanie finished for me.

I nodded along. "Right."

"Yeah, you guys can take turns being the knight so everyone gets to pick out what to do next." Melanie added.

The three of them seemed to agree and Milo finally stepped back. "Okay, the ladder is safe, but I have to check the bridge."

He took off in that direction while Finn and Alice waited at the top. Once he waved them on, they seemed happy to follow.

"Crisis averted." Melanie said with a wink.

I let out a sigh. "That was stressful."

We watched them as they crossed around the playground.

"You did a good job of figuring out a solution rather than just scolding them for fighting." She pointed at a mom who was begging her son to stop crying. "It's best to distract them with something new."

I'd have to remember that for next time.

7

BRANDON

Morning skate had been intense. Coach Romney and Rust were on us to keep the energy high and move quickly. We were playing the Boulder team, and tensions between us were at an all-time high. They considered us their rivals. We didn't think much of them, which drove them crazy. It didn't help that they had the most difficult arena and front office staff to work with. They always messed up our locker room, lost equipment or supplies, and only allowed for maybe two or three reserved tickets. For our entire team. Their behavior toward us had led to us never commenting on them in interviews. When the correspondents asked us about playing them or how the game went, we talked about something else. It was a long-standing joke that the rest of the league found entertaining. Well, everyone but Boulder. Not that we cared.

Every time we played them they would chirp at us, trying to make us mad or start a fight, but we blocked them out. Acted like they weren't on the ice. Then, we destroyed them.

As much as I disliked the team, I enjoyed these games for the extra challenge. Their hatred was palpable. They wanted so badly to affect us, but they didn't. Our lines had fun ignoring them while pushing them lower in the rankings.

"Ready, Dad?" Hartman asked as he passed me. "Rumor has it Turner has your name written on his glove."

I chuckled. Turner was a left defenseman that I took great pleasure in scoring on. It was happenstance that he was usually in my sweet spot.

"I can't wait." I headed to the locker room to change out for our warm-up before the game. I was halfway there when Amelia cut me off.

"Hey Cullen." She gave me a warm smile, but I was suspicious. We didn't normally stop and chat.

"Hi." I waited for her to say something, but when she didn't, I took another step toward the locker room.

"I was just wondering if things with the guys were any better today."

I twisted to look at her. "It was fine. Why?"

We'd been too focused for personal talks. My usual hecklers were exhausted by the time we were done practicing.

"I just noticed they were giving you a hard time the other day. Most of the guys are used to it, but you usually don't get involved."

She was worried about me? I almost laughed. "They didn't hurt my feelings. I'm just fine."

"Okay." She rolled her eyes. "I know I'm the new girl around here but that means I know how it feels to be on the outside. I don't want them scaring her away."

"She's just my boys' nanny."

Amelia ducked her head. "Never mind. You're right."

I stared at her until she finally met my eyes. She wasn't usually this involved with us outside of the training room. Oh no. This wasn't about the guys at all. "What do you know?"

She pursed her lips. "Nothing."

I lowered my voice. "Amelia."

"Ugh. Fine." She sighed. "Some of the Pride just mentioned that she was really nice."

I narrowed my eyes.

"And pretty."

I raised an eyebrow.

"And how she seems like a really good fit... for you."

She closed her eyes while I stared at the wall. Of course. I should have prepared myself for this. The women of the Pride were some of the most meddling, crafty, underhanded people I'd ever met. I loved most of them like family, but they were a terrifying force. They accomplished their goals no matter what. They were unapologetic and did whatever they thought was necessary. For the most part they used their powers for good. At least, from my perspective which was usually from a good distance away. For the past several years, I'd watched them matchmake and claw their way into the personal lives of several of my teammates, but since I'd been married, they'd left me alone.

That all changed when Olivia left. I became their newest project. They came into my home, into my life, and got to work. They were the reason I was able to continue to focus on my job and not miss a single practice, but they also felt that since they were semi-involved they—the Pride moved, thought, and acted as one after all—believed they had a vote in how I ran my life. My personal life.

Chloe knew someone who knew someone who helped me get the divorce done faster than usual in Utah. Not even a week had passed after my marriage was officially over that Madeline had a friend for me to meet. I refused, but that didn't discourage them. Multiple times a week, I was sent pictures of women they believed were a perfect fit.

It took a month for me to snap. I'd told them I wasn't ready and that they would be the very first I told when I was ready. It was the only way I could get them to back off.

I hadn't been tempted to break my silence on that front, until now. Until Sydney.

It was like they could sense the attraction I had to her. But none of them knew about that. *Except Amelia.*

I glared down at her and shook my head. I thought she was one of the good ones. "They got to you."

"I… ugh… Emma was already telling them how pretty she was and how she was laid back and just what you need."

The Pride could probably smell my vulnerability like predators. If I had any chance of keeping a hold on rumors, and not scaring Sydney away, I had to stop them before they got out of control.

"Tell them to stop."

She peeked up at me. "Please, please don't make me."

I narrowed my eyes. She was the newest. The weakling. I pitied her, for now. But she would have to learn to find her voice among the group eventually.

"Fine. I'll talk to Chloe," she sighed while shooting me one last pleading look.

"Talk to me about what."

I closed my eyes. Had I accidently said her name three times? Had I summoned her?

When I turned, Amelia was rushing back to the weight room. Coward. I guess it was up to me to lay down the law. Then pray she actually listened.

"I don't want you or any of the other women getting any ideas about Sydney and me. She's really good with the boys, and I don't want to ruin that."

Chloe tilted her head. "I agree. She's exactly what those boys need."

"Good. So you'll get any ideas of anything else happening out of your head?"

She grinned. "Fine. But that means you have to get them out of yours too."

I sighed. "Chloe. No."

"She called me today."

"What? Why? Was everything okay?" My heart was racing. I hadn't seen the boys all day, and other than a quick text from Sydney with a picture of the boys wearing their jerseys, I hadn't heard anything.

"Settle down, Dad. The boys wanted to go to the wood park but she had no idea what that was. I asked around and got her the location."

I shook my head. They did love that place. The gigantic castle could keep them busy for hours. That was sweet of her to find it. I should probably put together a list of their favorite places.

"Thanks for that."

Her eyes ran over my face. "She's a good one, Dad. I know neither of us know her all that well, but I like her." She took a step forward, bursting my personal bubble. "Don't mess it up."

With that vote of confidence, she turned and disappeared around a corner.

My shoulders dropped as the tension left me. I'd never, ever admit it aloud, but Chloe scared me. Not just in an intimidating way, but in a way that made me think if someone ever crossed her, she could make them go missing without a trace. She's the type that would get away with it too. She was that good. Plus, she had an army of eager minions to back up her dirty work.

"Dad! Come on." Olli hit his stick on the wall as he passed me. It was game time. I needed to focus.

I rushed through changing and stepped onto the ice a few minutes later. I took a lap around our team's half while stretching my shoulders and arms. There were already crowds against the glass shouting and slamming their hands to get our attention. I smiled and nodded at a few groups but paused when I saw two of my favorite faces beaming up at me.

I stopped and pulled out my mouth guard. "Hey guys."

"Dad!" they shouted together.

"You guys excited?" I shouted over the sound of people cheering around them.

They both nodded before Milo pointed over his shoulder. "It's Sydney's first game."

I looked behind them and nearly fell over. She was in my jersey. Her long, sun kissed hair was draped over one shoulder and she waved at me. "Good luck!"

I couldn't help but smile wider. "Thanks."

Chloe stood next to her, wiggling her fingers with a wicked smile. I nearly threw my hands in the air. How had she made it across the arena that fast? That woman was everywhere.

If there was more time, I would have told them to come to the tunnel, but I really needed to get my head right. I couldn't be thinking about Sydney while also delivering a humiliating defeat to the team who shall not be named.

"I'll see you guys after."

All three of them nodded and waved as I turned and headed to start the drills. I joined the line as we took shots at Olli, letting muscle memory take over.

It had been fifteen years since I joined the NHL. I'd been an eighteen-year-old straight out of high school. I'd been nervous back then, but more excited about the chance to prove myself.

Tonight was the first time in my professional career I was nervous because of the audience. Even with Olivia, I was more excited about showing off to her. Proud to know she was watching me. Well, I quickly learned that attending the games didn't mean she was watching. She was usually taking pictures of herself and her friends hanging out in a suite, or networking with someone she deemed important enough.

This was different. Sydney was different.

It was dumb; I wanted to impress her. I wanted her to

enjoy the game, maybe even get her to fall in love with the sport. The boys always begged to come to as many games as possible, but Olivia didn't like taking them with her. They took her attention away from what she needed to be doing, being seen or networking or whatever it was she did.

Sydney wasn't Olivia, and I couldn't be more grateful for that. I knew she would dote on the boys tonight and make sure they had everything they needed and wanted during the game. If they wanted to come to more, she would bring them, but I wanted her to have fun too.

Hopefully the Pride was on their best behavior tonight. They could be intense, so I had to pray the full force of them didn't push Sydney away.

I took a shot at Olli, but he blocked it. On my way back to the line I scanned the area where the Pride sat and found the boys front and center with Sydney and Chloe next to them. *Good.* As much as she scared the guys, Chloe would make sure Sydney felt welcome. As the unofficial ring leader, she held a lot of sway about who was accepted into the group. She didn't like women she suspected were using any of us guys. She could practically sniff out the jersey chasers and made sure they didn't stay around long. Some thought her ruthless, but she had each of our best interests at heart. She didn't want any of us, or the team, getting hurt.

I'd watched from afar as Madeline, Colby, Kendall, Lucy, Addison, Elena, and Amelia came into the fold. Chloe was different with them from the beginning. It was like she intuitively knew who the right ones were. Who was going to end up together for the long haul.

Sydney wasn't here for me, though. She was here for the boys. Of course, Chloe and the rest of the women would include her. There was no threat. She was a neutral zone.

I took another shot and then glanced back up in the crowd. Sydney was bent over talking to Finn. I watched as she gave him her full attention and then nodded. Finn's grin widened, and Sydney was pulled into a conversation with Emma who just arrived with Jackson. I loved the way she really listened to the boys. She didn't patronize them. What they had to say and what they needed was just as valid as any adult.

She was so great.

"Stop staring." Erik tapped his stick against my shin. "You're being too obvious."

"I'm making sure the boys are okay."

He rolled his eyes. "No, you're not. They're surrounded by like twenty women who dote on them and get them anything they want. They're more taken care of here than anywhere else. You're watching *her*."

I shot him a look and turned away to ignore him.

"Who's the new girl?" Dallin, one of the rookies, said while staring up at the Pride.

"I don't know. She's hot though," Jason said. "She's too old for you though. She needs a mature man."

"Like you?" Reese said with a laugh.

Jason glared at him. "Yeah, actually."

I pushed him aside and cut him off. "Both of you leave her alone. She's my kids' nanny."

Jason's eyebrows shot up. "The one you like?"

"What? No." I shook my head. I forgot he'd been in the weight room at the time the guys all laid into me. "Just stay away."

They smirked and I almost hit them, but that would just make things worse and encourage the rumors that I was interested in her.

8

SYDNEY

The energy in the arena was more intense than I would have ever dreamed. It was like a buzz that started out dull when we first got there, and the boys said we needed to go down to the glass first. It had been thirty minutes before the start time, and there were only a few pockets of people. As the countdown got lower and lower and the seats filled, the buzz grew until I could feel it in my veins.

The moment the teams finished the pre-game stuff and the puck dropped, the energy in the arena went from a five to off the charts. There was music and screaming and the action on the ice was lightning fast. This was no baseball game.

I didn't know where to look. The puck moved faster than I could track it, yet somehow the players were always exactly where they needed to be.

My awe grew when Hartman—Finn pointed out the captain at the very beginning— scored in the first three minutes. I had no idea it would be this exciting. I suddenly resented the years of watching baseball and football on TV, believing these were the ultimate sports to watch. *Oh Dad. You are missing out.*

I wanted to call him. I wanted to tell him all about it. I wanted him to know I understood him just a little bit more. If his sports made him feel even the tiniest bit of what I was feeling now, I got it.

"Look! Erik!" Milo shouted and pointed to the player racing across the ice with the puck. There was no one around him. The nearest opponent was several strides behind him. He swung his stick and hit the puck into the top of the net.

"Yes Erik!" Chloe screamed, and Madeline, who I just met, was smiling and crying. She rubbed her belly, and I couldn't help but giggle. Pregnancy hormones seemed to be taking over.

It was adorable that the sisters-in-law were both pregnant at the same time. Emma joked that Erik and Chloe did everything together, so it was destined to happen. Madeline just shook her head and shrugged.

"He's a good scorer," Milo said with a definitive nod.

"That's Noah. He's defense." Finn pointed at another padded giant. I read Malkin on his back and tried to commit that to memory. It was so confusing when the women called half the guys by their first name and the other half by their last. The boys seemed to call everyone by their first name, except Hartman. Actually, I didn't hear anyone refer to the captain as anything but that. Maybe... unless I didn't put it together.

"What's Hartman's first name?" I leaned over to ask Emma.

"Wyatt." She answered. "Why?"

"The boys use first names, but everyone else seems to use a mix. I'm just trying to keep everyone straight."

She laughed. "Yeah, sorry about that. The guys mostly use

last names. We usually use first, like the boys." She paused. "Then again, that's not always true. I guess it depends on the guy. Only Coach calls Olli, my husband, Letang. Everyone else calls him Olli. Reese is fifty-fifty. For Erik," she laughed again, "it depends on if he's in trouble or not."

"Great, that's super helpful," I said with a sigh.

She smiled and shook her head. "I know. Sorry we created such a mess. Just give it time. You'll catch on. It's not like someone will laugh at you for calling them by their first name. Or last." She paused. "Really, either way, they'll respond."

I laughed. That made things even more confusing. I was going to have to take some time to memorize the roster. I picked up on Brandon talking about Rust and Romney and realized they were the coaches pretty quickly. At least I had them straight.

The women were another challenge. It was easy enough for them to learn my name, but it was overwhelming to take them all in, let alone pair them with their player. Not all of them were wearing jerseys, so I couldn't even cheat and peek at the number or name.

Since the game started there wasn't much of a chance to chat anyway. I was sitting with Chloe, Emma, and Madeline, who were with Reese, Olli, and Erik. That was all I needed to remember for right now.

"I have to pee," Finn announced.

"Okay, let's go up." I stood and took his hand to lead him down the row. "Milo, do you need to go?"

He broke his concentration on the game long enough to think about it and jump out of his seat. "Yeah!"

"Excuse us." I stepped past Madeline and Emma as fast as I could so I didn't block their view. "Which way is the closest restroom?"

"Make a left," they said at the same time.

"Come on, boys." They ran up the stairs ahead of me, but waited at the portal entrance. "This way." I directed them to the left, and luckily there was a women's restroom just a few feet away. Was this why the Pride sat in this section? It had to have influenced their decision.

The boys each ran into their own stalls the moment we walked in. "Wait at the sinks if you finish before me."

They didn't reply, so I hurried before rushing out to wash my hands. They were both stretching to reach the soap so I gave them a boost before walking them over to dry off. This was our first public restroom experience, and it had gone smoother than I expected. I didn't want to try to coordinate this when there was a massive line in here though. Hopefully, they wouldn't need to go during the breaks between quarters. Periods? Halves? Oh boy. I didn't even know the basics.

"All set?"

"Yeah!" They set out toward the exit when a blond in high heels and a skin-tight Fury shirt walked in. They almost ran into her but stopped in time.

"Hey! Watch it!" she screeched. Then she looked down at them and a fake smile spread across her face. "Oh, hello boys."

They took a step back from her but didn't seem scared.

"I haven't seen you guys in so long." She bent down a few inches. "How's your mommy?"

The twins shared an apprehensive look before staring at the ground. Who was this woman? Was she with the Pride? I didn't recognize her, but the introductions had all been so brief I could have forgotten.

I didn't like that she was bothering them, though. I hadn't brought up their mom because they never did. They weren't shy about saying everything that went through their minds, so until they mentioned her, I wouldn't.

"Come on, guys." I tried to move between them and the stranger but she blocked me.

"Who are you?" she asked as if I were about to kidnap the boys. "Boys, you should come with me."

I stared back at her, stunned by her catty attitude and her bold suggestion.

They took a step back, hitting my legs. "I don't think so."

"Sydney, would you mind holding this for me?" Madeline walked into the bathroom holding out a large soda and squeezed past me without paying any attention to the other woman. "I had a craving for a root beer, but as soon as I got it I had to pee. Of course." She laughed and walked a few steps away before finally turning to face the very disgruntled woman. "Move on, leech."

I nearly broke out laughing. I'd never seen such an indignant look as when the woman flung her hair over her shoulder and stormed out.

I almost laughed until I saw Madeline's expression. "Who was that?"

Her eyes dipped to the boys. "One of *her* friends."

Oh. Right. That made a lot of sense. Madeline had been nothing but sweet until now. I made a mental note to never cross her. "Got it."

She went into a stall and we waited for her, dutifully holding her precious root beer. Once we were on our way back, the boys ran down the stairs while I took them slower with Madeline.

"Olivia didn't sit with us. She never really made an effort to get to know any of the women in the Pride. She sat up in one of the suites with her friends and people she deemed worthy of her time."

I wanted to ask more but now wasn't the time. "Thanks for stepping in."

"Anytime." She smiled and we scooted through the aisle back to our seats.

"Look, Daddy has the puck!" Finn shouted.

I found him on the ice just in time to see him swing and

shoot the puck past the goalie. We all jumped to our feet, screaming and cheering for him. The guys on the ice surrounded him, clapping him on the back and the helmet.

"That was amazing," I said and the boys clapped. Seeing Brandon in his element was surreal. Sure, I figured he was a good player. You didn't become a professional athlete if you weren't, but seeing him in action was completely different. He was so smooth, so natural. He made it look effortless, like I could lace up some skates and hit a tiny puck past an enormous man.

I couldn't believe we almost missed that.

The boys were standing on their seats cheering proudly for their dad. He turned and pointed up at them which only made them cheer louder.

The crowd around us all turned and started staring at them, well, us. I realized then that I was with the boys, cheering like a madwoman in his jersey. Oh no. What did that look like to the outside world?

I quickly sat down and hoped I'd go unnoticed. The last thing I wanted was for rumors to start and add to the stress Brandon carried around every day.

"You'll get used to it." Emma squeezed my knee. "Brandon will need to make it known you're the boys' nanny, and people will move on."

I wasn't sure I believed there would ever come a time when I'd be used to people staring at me. Had I been ignorant to think Brandon's career wouldn't affect me? It wasn't like we were ever together, at least not in public. I spent my time with the boys. People shouldn't put us together, but that wasn't how it felt right now. I felt like the entire arena was staring at me. Assuming.

I wasn't bothered by it, except for the impact it could have on Brandon. He was dealing with enough. I knew how ruthless people could be, especially with celebrities, and

Brandon might not act like it, but he was one. I checked his social media accounts. I knew his assistant ran them, but he had over two million followers. People loved him. He'd been a rock in the league for a long time. He was a household hockey name.

I still wasn't sure how I managed to meet him without figuring it out. I guess that turned out to be a blessing. But now, my eyes were open to his fame. I knew how far his influence reached. His fans cared about him as a person as much as they cared about him as a player. They were devastated for him when he broke the news of his separation then divorce. They wanted him to be happy. They wanted him to move on.

Then for them to see me. With the boys. Wearing his jersey. Sitting with the wives and girlfriends of the players.

Of course people would jump to the first conclusion.

Maybe it wasn't that big of a deal. Only the people around us noticed. Right? It wasn't like this would even leave the building. Give it ten minutes and someone else would score and they'd forget all about this mortifying moment.

Maybe I should get a jersey made that said "nanny." I almost smiled. Now *that* wouldn't get people talking.

"Sydney, look!" Finn pointed to the corner of the ice across from us. "Olli has the puck!"

I watched the goalie take the puck from the corner while all of the other players were on the opposite side of the ice from him. He looked back and forth before hitting it to one of his teammates. I couldn't read the jersey to see who it was.

"Noah's gonna hit it," Milo said with confidence. I wasn't sure if Noah was even on the ice, but these boys had been right so far, so I didn't question them. They were pretty good with the rules and following the game. Better than I expected for four-year-olds, but I guess when your dad was a player it was in your blood.

"That's awesome," I said, wanting to be encouraging but not quite knowing what was going on. I needed to focus on them and making sure they were having fun, not worrying about what other people might be thinking.

9

BRANDON

The boys were usually good about letting me sleep in the morning after a game. And by sleep in, I mean they left me alone for an extra thirty minutes, so when I opened my eyes to a dark room, I had to think about where I was.

Hotel room? No, last night was at home. Where were the cartoons? The boys' laughter?

I rolled over and checked my clock. It was nearly nine already. I couldn't remember the last time they stayed in bed that long, not without being sick.

Oh no. I jumped out of bed and pulled on a pair of pants as I hurried out of my room and down the hall. Their door was open, and their room quiet.

"Boys?" I stepped in, looking at their beds. "Milo? Finn?"

I went to the playroom, but it was empty, too. Where were they?

I started down the stairs and nearly jumped to the bottom when I heard their voices. I rushed into the kitchen and froze. Sydney stood at the stove, wearing a pair of boxers and an oversized shirt. Her hair was piled on top of her head, and she was smiling as she listened to Milo's story.

I committed this moment to memory. It was perfection. A beautiful woman smiling, makeup-free, not worried about anything other than my boys. They were sitting on the edge of the counter on the island so they could watch her while she moved around the kitchen. She listened as the boys told her about a dinosaur show they watched last week.

"So the Brontosaurus is the big one with the long neck?"

Milo nodded. "They eat plants."

"How do they get that big eating plants?" she asked.

Finn shrugged. "Dad tells us we have to eat vegetables to grow big. They do it."

She smiled. "That's right. But that's not your favorite, right?"

"No! Mine's a Stegosaurus!" Finn formed a horn with his hands on his head and started imitating what I assumed was the noise they made.

She clapped. "That was so good. I thought one was in the house!"

Finn's chest puffed up. "We practice a lot at school."

I could tell she was holding back laughter. "That's amazing. Milo, can you do your favorite?"

He nodded and held his arms up close to his body. "I'm a Velociraptor."

His squeal-growls were louder than necessary, but she didn't seem to mind.

"Oh that's a scary one isn't it."

He nodded. "They're carnivores."

"Brontosaurus are nice though. That can be your favorite." Finn offered.

"That's perfect." She made a noise between a meow and growl and they all broke out laughing.

This was what the boys deserved. This was what they should've always had.

How had I let myself think that Olivia's behavior was okay? She put herself first one hundred percent of the time.

She didn't pause to listen to her sons. She pushed them off on someone else whenever she could. She never cooked for them, not unless she was filming a video to show off how amazing she was at being the perfect mom. She would never be caught without her hair, make up, and outfit perfectly coordinated. She was fake. I should have seen it years ago. I was too busy justifying everything. I was a master of talking myself into things, cutting her slack, and ignoring everything that was wrong with our relationship.

"Daddy!" Finn waved at me, and I moved to them so they didn't try to jump off the counters.

"There are my boys. I thought you ran away." I hugged them both tight and soaked in the sound of their giggles. It was the perfect balm to my sore body. I didn't recover as quickly as I did when I was a rookie, but having them around to distract me and keep me moving was more than I could ask for.

"No Daddy! Sydney came and got us so we could make pancakes. We were going to bring you breakfast in bed but you woke up," Milo explained.

Sydney waved her spatula in the air. "You ruined the surprise."

She turned to look at me for the first time and fell against the stove. The way her jaw dropped just a bit gave me way too much satisfaction. I stood still, allowing her to get her eyeful. She seemed stuck on my abs, so I twisted just a bit away from the boys so she had a better view.

I couldn't help it. I was a man who hadn't had this kind of attention in a very long time. In the back of my mind a voice was screaming, *She's the nanny!* But I didn't care.

"Sorry guys. I'll try to sleep longer next time."

My voice seemed to break the spell she was under. Her face went bright pink and she spun to face the stove. I smirked and looked at the boys.

"We'll be faster next time," Finn said with determination.

"Sounds good. Did you guys have fun last night?"

I watched as they nodded before I peeked at Sydney. Her back was still to me so I couldn't see her expression.

"Yeah, we saw your goal and we cheered real loud for you." Milo waved his hands around.

"Thanks, boys. That means so much to me. I loved knowing you guys were there watching."

"Can we go again, Daddy?"

I looked at Sydney, taking in her legs while I had a chance. "Hopefully soon. It's up to Sydney."

She turned and smiled, still looking a bit flustered. "When's the next home game?"

"We're leaving in a few days for a three-game trip, so it will be next week."

"Oh yeah. Right." She spun and hurried to flip a pancake.

"We can go next week!" Finn told Milo as if he hadn't been listening.

"Yay!"

I waited for Sydney to correct them or tell them they would have to wait and see. She didn't. She smiled at them and joined in the little happy dance the boys were doing. "We should try the pretzels next time. Remember how big they were?"

Milo lifted his hands to frame his face. "As big as my head."

Sydney nodded. "Yeah, we're going to see if we can finish it."

This woman was amazing. She was incredible with the boys. It had been less than a week and I was already dreading the thought of her leaving next year.

Sydney dished out pancakes onto four plates and told the boys to get on their chairs so we could eat. She set the plates out in front of them and made sure they were taken care of before offering a plate to me.

"Do you want to put a shirt on before eating?" she asked while maintaining perfect eye contact.

"Nah, I'm good." I grinned and took the plate.

"Sure." She cleared her throat. "That was a really great game yesterday. I wasn't sure what to expect, but I had a lot of fun."

I started down at my Mickey Mouse pancakes and laughed. Of course she made designs. "I'm glad."

"There was one thing that happened." She was watching the boys, who were distracted with their food, and her voice was quiet.

"What?" My mind ran through a million possibilities.

"We had a run-in with someone while taking a bathroom break."

That was unexpected. "What do you mean? With a fan?"

She shook her head. "No, I think she's a friend of your ex. They boys seemed to know her, but didn't like her much."

My stomach dropped. I should have warned her that some of Olivia's lackies were still around.

"Sorry about that."

She shrugged one shoulder. "Madeline came in and got rid of her. It was just weird because she tried to get the boys to go with her. They didn't, and I wouldn't have let them, obviously, but it was just strange."

That was weird. I wondered who it was, but they were all the same to me.

"Thanks for taking care of them. I'll remind security to keep an eye out when you guys are there."

She nodded and took a big bite of her syrupy pancake. She sighed and closed her eyes. "So good."

I took a bite and grunted in agreement. They were light, fluffy, and delicious. "I could get used to this."

She elbowed my arm and shook her head. "Don't get too excited. My cooking abilities are perfect for the palates of four-year-olds, but once they get past the mac and cheese and peanut butter sandwiches phase I'm out of luck."

I chuckled, pretending like her casual touch was completely normal and nothing to obsess over. "Don't worry. I'm thirty-three and still in that phase."

She laughed and moved to make sure the boys were eating. "Do you want another one, Milo?"

He nodded quickly. "Yes, please."

Whoa. Not only was he eating, but he had manners? Was this the twilight zone?

"Good job, buddy."

He grinned at me and Finn jumped in. "Me too, Sydney. One more, please."

I watched as she set the pancakes on their plates then moved back next to me.

"Thank you!" they said together.

I narrowed my eyes at her. "Okay, are you secretly Mary Poppins?"

She cocked her head. "What?"

"You have them eating real food, which is a miracle, and they're saying please and thank you?"

She shrugged. "I cannot reveal my secrets."

"Oh right." I took another bite and watched the boys in wonder.

Last week, we'd been living in chaos. I was usually yelling at them to get dressed or out the door. We survived on premade meals or fast food. They threw tantrums daily, and I was stressed to the max.

Sydney changed everything. They were so much happier and better behaved. They listened and were polite. It was hard not to blame myself, but I'd been doing my best. It just wasn't enough. She came at the perfect time and pushed a reset button. The guilt about them not having their mother was lessening. Olivia didn't deserve them. She'd walked away. She chose herself over her sons.

This was the childhood they needed. Full of pancakes and playing and learning.

I turned to her as I reached for another pancake. "Thank you."

She met my eyes and didn't ask what I meant. She just gave me a small smile. "No, thank you."

There was something about how she said those words that made me pause. She managed to seamlessly become a part of our world, but I still didn't know very much about her.

Maybe she needed us as much as we needed her.

I barely walked into the locker room before I was assaulted with phones, papers, and shouts.

Hartman pulled my elbow and moved us out of the way. "You have some explaining to do."

"What are you talking about?"

He lifted his phone and showed me a picture of Sydney standing and clapping with the boys next to her. The headline read 'Cullen's New Mystery Woman.' I didn't bother to read it.

"I can't control the press."

He gave me an exasperated look. "I'm well aware. I just think you should clarify who she is before they set up their cameras at your house."

He was probably right. I wasn't the most famous guy on the team, and I tried to lay low as much as possible, but unfortunately, I had enough of a fanbase that even the Hollywood tabloids picked up the story of my divorce. I was pretty sure Olivia was behind that and wanted to use the exposure to make herself more relevant. All it did was make me angry.

I was fine doing interviews and photoshoots. I was more than happy to meet fans and personally respond to their letters and emails. I drew the line at my family. I didn't want the boys to be impacted by their mother's and my actions and decisions. I wanted to stop this before it got out of control.

Instead of changing for practice, I spun around and headed up to the front office. Chloe's office door was open, so I knocked on the frame before stepping inside and sitting down.

She glanced up at me for a second before returning to her laptop. Her hands flew over the keyboard, not wavering for a moment.

"I already saw it."

"I don't want to issue a formal statement, but I want them to know she's the boys' nanny."

Her fingers finally stopped, and she faced me. "I'll get the word out. I'm not as connected with the tabloids as the sports news, but I'll see what I can do."

"Thanks." I stood to leave, but she put up her hand.

"This isn't going to fix everything."

I slumped down. "Why not?"

She looked at me like I was an idiot. "She's a hot nanny. You're a newly single man. There will be plenty of rumors and lies."

I rolled my eyes at the cliché, but she wasn't wrong.

"For all we know, Olivia will take it and spin it. She could make claims that Sydney is why you guys split. Why you're keeping the boys from her."

"What? Chloe, that's insane."

She sighed. "I know that. The media doesn't, nor do they care as long as it sells and makes them money."

"I didn't even know Sydney two weeks ago."

"I'm aware, and we have plenty of proof of that. Sydney wasn't even in Utah. We can dispel the rumors as they come, but we can't prevent them from starting."

"Can we stop Olivia before she says anything?"

She laughed. "As much as I'd love to put a muzzle on that one, we can't get a gag order without going to court."

I pinched the bridge of my nose. I made it a stipulation of the divorce that she couldn't write a book or publish anything about our marriage. I should have included leaking anything to the press. I'd naively thought she wouldn't do anything to hurt the boys, but a story like this was exactly the kind of thing she'd use to her advantage.

"We'll get this under control. Just be patient. Things will blow over."

She was the master of public relations, so I had to believe her. "Thanks, Chloe."

My ex had taken enough from me. I stood back and let her have the last word, cast me as the villain, and control the narrative to her followers. I wasn't going to let her or anyone else hurt Sydney, though. She was an innocent in the battle between Olivia and me.

Hopefully, Chloe would get the truth out and people would lose interest. There wasn't much to the story. We didn't get to spend time together, at least not outside of the house. We were too boring for people to care for very long.

The only thing I could do was make sure she and the boys were left alone. I didn't want this getting anywhere near Milo and Finn. They'd been through enough. I didn't want to scare them, but if the media became a problem, I wasn't going to have a choice.

10

SYDNEY

Four straight days with the boys felt daunting when Brandon left, but it flew by. We called him every day so they could see him and tell him all about their days. Over the weekend we went to the museum, and since the weather was nice, we spent almost ten hours at the zoo.

By the end of the day, I told the boys they were going to go on exhibit if we didn't leave. Their energy was never on short supply. They ran from one animal to the next, circling back to their favorites until my feet ached. They did sleep in the next morning, so at least I had that small miracle.

I also got my first paycheck in my account. After doing a little happy dance and taking the boys to preschool, I put together everything I needed for a passport and submitted my application. It was the first step toward my dream. In six to eight weeks, I'd be free to go anywhere I wanted. Well, technically I had to wait for my contract to end, but soon I would have options. That was more than I could say for the past ten years.

Since the weather was still nice and warm, I told the boys we were having a pool party after school. I checked to make sure the water was warm enough and was pleasantly surprised to discover it was heated. No wonder it was uncovered in March.

I made popsicles and sandwiches and found the controls for the outdoor speakers so we could have music too. I even found their little swim trunks so all they had to do was change and put on sunscreen before play time. I changed into my most modest swimsuit, a baby blue crochet one piece, and went to pick them up.

They were in such good moods and raced each other to get ready and meet me on the patio to get lathered so their pale skin didn't burn.

"Are you guys ready?"

They nodded in synchronization. "Yay!"

"Okay, let's get those floaties on." I tugged them onto their arms while they wiggled, too anxious to get in the water.

Milo ran to the edge, jumping in without pausing, while Finn waited for his brother to surface. "Watch out!"

He made sure he had plenty of room before jumping in. They took off, swimming toward the waterfall and cave under the slides. They made it to a bench and took turns jumping through the curtain, making funny faces at me each time.

I couldn't stop smiling. They were so happy and excited to show me all their tricks. They begged me to get in the water with them, so I did a cannonball which earned me a standing ovation and endless giggles.

"You made a super splash!" Finn threw his arms in the air. "It went this high."

"I want to try!" Milo doggie paddled across the pool to the stairs and hurried to the side of the pool, lining up across from Finn and me.

His eyes locked on mine, and I nodded. "You got this."

He beamed and jumped, barely reaching around his knees with the floaties in the way. His little splash was precious. I couldn't stop my laugh from escaping. His head bobbed while he waited for our reactions.

"It was so big, Milo!" Finn threw his arms out wide. "Now it's my turn!"

He went through the same motions, waiting for me to tell him to go before jumping and tucking his knees. He landed on his back but didn't seem to mind.

"Was it big?" he sputtered.

Milo jumped on the bench. "So big!"

That seemed to be the highest form of praise in their minds so I echoed, "So, so big!"

Finn smiled and swam over to us. "Let's go on the slide, Milo."

They took off to the other end, and I moved across the pool so I could watch them.

When they reached the top of the smaller slide they both looked to the house and squealed. "Daddy!"

I spun and saw Brandon walking toward us in his trunks. "You're having a party without me?" he said in fake anger with his hands on his hips.

They giggled and nodded their heads.

"And going on the slide without me?"

Milo shrugged. "It was Sydney's idea."

Sure, kid. Throw me under the bus. Brandon looked down at me with a wicked smile before taking a step back. He ran and did a cannonball right in front of me, causing a wave to wash over me.

I was wiping my eyes when he came up grinning. "Oh, sorry. Did I get you?"

I shrugged a shoulder and swam a few feet away. "I didn't notice."

Being this close to him while he was basically half-naked wasn't easy. The last thing I wanted was to get caught staring. Well, again. I was pretty sure he noticed me ogling him in the kitchen the other morning.

But this was more than anyone could handle. He was larger than life with muscles in places I didn't know could grow muscles. Like that neck? I blew out a breath and focused on the boys.

Milo went down the slide followed by Finn, and they went to their dad asking him to throw them.

He had them climb onto his shoulders one at time and then launched them into the deep end. Each time, they surfaced laughing harder and harder. When Finn started choking from too much excitement and not enough breathing, I told them it was time for sandwiches. They got out and sat at the end of the lounge chairs, adorably wrapped up in towels while eating.

I got back in the water with Brandon, who was leaning against the edge, his arms stretched out on either side of him. It was quite the view. I didn't think muscles could really look like that, not outside of superhero movies.

And his chest.

Songs could be written about that chest.

"Sydney?"

My eyes trailed up his thick neck, wet lips, and I finally realized he was watching me. "Huh?"

"I said thanks for doing this. They're having a blast."

He'd spoken and I didn't hear him? Oh no. He definitely knew I was checking him out. *Bad Sydney.*

"No problem. I'm having fun too."

He smiled and dropped his head back, soaking in the sun. "I needed this."

He was doing this on purpose. He knew he was attractive, and flaunting it in front of me was just cruel.

I cleared my throat. "How was the trip?"

"Long, but good." He sighed and met my gaze. "I missed you guys."

Not the boys. You guys. Me included?

I could tell myself that it didn't mean anything, but it mattered, at least to me.

"We missed you too." There. We. I volleyed back to him, letting him take control. He could steer this in whatever direction he wanted.

"Oh did you?"

I nodded. "We had a good time, but it would have been fun to have you there."

He ducked his head. "That's one of the hardest parts about my job. I miss out on so much."

"I don't think they see it like that. They miss you, sure, but they're so proud of you. We watched all the games and they cheered you on like crazy. I think they understand it's your job, but when you're home, you're there for them."

"I'm trying."

"You're doing a pretty good job." It seemed like he needed that reassurance quite a bit. He told me before he hired me that he wanted to do better for them. I could tell he was doing his very best, and if the boys didn't already know that, they would eventually.

"Thanks, Syd."

That was the first time he'd called me that. It felt familiar. Personal. I tried not to react.

"Anytime, Dad." I caught on to the nickname at the game and waited for the perfect time to use it.

He cringed. "Not you too."

I laughed. "I can't call you that. It's too weird."

"Thank you. I get enough of it from the team."

"Is it weird being one of the older guys on the team?" I'd done the math and he was only a few years older than me, but according to my research in the NHL, that was a veteran age.

"It does feel like the rookies get younger and younger each year while I stay the same, but then again, it feels like

I've been playing forever. Way longer than just thirteen years."

"I can't believe all you've done," I paused. "You've accomplished so much."

His eyes searched my face. "And living in like thirty different cities isn't something to brag about?"

"Forty-five."

His brows shot up. "Really?"

I nodded. "I told you I moved a lot."

"Yeah." He blew out a breath. "I guess I didn't realize what an understatement that was. What's been your favorite?"

"Each city was a new, exciting experience. There were times when I found good, stable jobs that required a normal forty hour work week. I didn't love those as much as when I had more free time. I was a waitress in New Orleans during Mardi Gras. That was an unforgettable experience." I smiled at the wild nights that seemed to last forever. "But if I had to narrow it down to the top three, I'd say Pittsburgh, Savanna, and Key West."

"That's quite a diverse group."

"It's all about the people." I tiled my head toward the sun. "They make all the difference."

"I agree," he said thoughtfully. "I've heard of teams that hated each other, or had rivalries or drama with the guys. I can't imagine having to live with that. It would make playing more of a chore and truly a job rather than my passion. I'm lucky the Fury is my home because we have such a great dynamic. We're truly a family."

"You are lucky you found that."

He stared at me for a moment. "What do you want?"

"What do you mean?" I glanced away. "That's a loaded question."

"Committing to staying here seemed hard on you. You want to continue to travel and move around. Why?"

I already told him about wanting to see the world, but I guess I didn't tell him the whole story. "I grew up on the same street both my parents did. My mom's parents lived two blocks south, and my dad's parents lived on the other side of town. None of them left; they didn't ever want to. Their whole world exists within a twenty-mile radius." Just the thought of my hometown made me feel claustrophobic. "It was the kind of place people never got out of, and I couldn't stand that possibility. I left the first day I could and never looked back. I didn't want to get trapped. I wanted to see everything. Experience as much as I could. I want to be a part of the world."

He didn't say anything for a minute. "I understand that. I get to see and do more than a lot of people because of my job, but at the same time, I don't have very much control over what happens. I could get traded, or injured, and things would completely change."

I cringed. "That's terrifying."

"It can be, but I don't focus on that. I just do my best to appreciate what I have right now."

His eyes lingered on my face and I felt my whole body warm.

"I'm done," Finn announced and broke free of his towel. Milo followed a few seconds later, and they both jumped into the pool.

We played together for a few hours before the boys got bored and wanted popsicles. Brandon and I didn't get any more alone time together, but I couldn't be bothered by that. I wasn't here for him. The stolen moments were nice, and I definitely savored them, but my attention was meant for Milo and Finn.

After we all showered and cleaned up, I searched the fridge for something to cook for dinner.

"Looking for ideas?" Brandon came up behind me, nearly pressing his body against mine. So close I could feel his warmth.

"Ah. Yeah, but I can give you guys some space if you want some alone time with them." I turned enough to see his face. His eyes trailed up my body before reaching my eyes.

"No. Stay. I'll grill burgers, if you want."

I nodded and tried to move out of the way, but I was boxed in. His arm slid across mine as he reached in and pulled out the meat.

He finally stepped back, and I heard the back door open. I could finally breathe. I wasn't sure if this was all in my mind, or if he was purposely teasing me.

Everything was innocent enough. Of course he was going to be shirtless while swimming, and I might have just been in the way. He could have asked me to move instead of rubbing against me, but I didn't mind.

I was losing it. Definitely. He wasn't interested in me like that. He saw me as his sons' nanny.

One year. I just had to survive one year, and then I was off to my grand adventure. No getting attached. I had to remember that. All of this was temporary.

"I forgot to give this to you." His voice made me jump. I hadn't heard him come back inside. When I turned, he had an envelope for me.

"What is it?" My name was handwritten beautifully on the front.

"I'm not sure. Emma asked me to give it to you."

I broke the seal and pulled out a silver and teal baby shower invitation. "Oh wow."

I would have never expected to be invited. She and the Pride had been great about including me at the game, but this was a personal thing.

"What is it?" Brandon peered over my shoulder.

"I'm invited to Chloe's baby shower this weekend."

He huffed out a laugh. "I can pretend I forgot to give it to you if you want."

I gasped. "No way. It's so sweet that they included me."

He shrugged. "Careful, they'll pull you into the dark side."

I laughed and rolled my eyes. "You're very dramatic."

He held up his hands. "Just offering you a way out. I know those women can be a lot to take, especially when they're all together. Don't come back crying, saying I didn't warn you."

"What do you think is going to happen at a baby shower?"

"You never know with them." He walked back outside shaking his head.

He might not understand or appreciate it, but this was huge for me. They were offering friendship. Inclusion into a pretty exclusive group.

I hadn't been exaggerating when I said that the people made the place. I was going to be here for a year, so I might as well enjoy it as much as I could.

But no getting attached.

11

BRANDON

I was pushing the limits. I knew it and I had a feeling Sydney did too. It started out as an accident. When I ran downstairs shirtless looking for the boys, I forgot a shirt because my mind was focused on making sure they hadn't escaped. Her reaction turned it into something more.

The way she drank me in while we were swimming was enough to push me over the edge. If the boys weren't there. If she didn't work for me. If a million other factors were different, I would have made a move.

Divorced. Dad. Old man.

She was making me lose my mind. Making me forget who I was. The various labels that weighed me down. My never-ending responsibilities. She made me forget all of that. She saw *me*.

It was impossible to ignore that feeling. There were a million reasons I should, and I repeated them to myself over and over daily. Every time I got a handle on it, she did something to make my resolve crumble all over again.

Playing games with the boys. Anticipating their requests long before they had a chance to ask. Hugging them. Joking with them. Smiling while she watched them when she thought no one was around.

She was genuine. Raw. She didn't pretend to be anything other than herself, and she never apologized for it.

I knew there was a timer hanging over us. She was counting down the days until she could leave and live out her dreams. I had to decide between enjoying the time with her while she was here, or shut off my heart until she was gone.

Both options sucked.

I was selfish. One month and I never wanted her to leave. I wanted her to want to be here. But how could I ask that of her? She was already outside her comfort zone, staying here until next spring. I couldn't get in the way of her dreams. Not as someone who knew the sacrifices it took to reach them.

So my decision was to not make a decision.

I could simply enjoy what was happening now, which happened to include playing with the boys and Sydney.

They came up with a new game. Well, an obstacle course that went from their bedroom to the playroom. Sydney helped build it while I was at practice a few days ago, and I helped make a few tweaks to meet the boys' specifications.

It was their newest obsession, though I knew those tended to only last a few days. We would enjoy it while it lasted.

"My turn!" Milo shouted as he ran to the top of the landing in the fake trees in their room.

"I'll time you." Sydney held up her phone, and when he was ready, started the clock.

They had to army crawl across the landing, walk one foot in front of the other across the bridge, then climb down the ladder. The rules on the ground were a bit foggy—I was pretty sure they changed each round—but there was usually some hopscotch, spinning, jumping on one leg, and crab walks.

All that mattered was that the boys were thrilled and burning some energy. The bonus was that so far they hadn't asked Sydney or me to participate. We simply had to watch and keep a record of their times. This was my favorite kind of activity.

"Go Milo, go!" Finn ran along with his brother cheering him on. I loved that they didn't compete. They just encouraged each other. I knew someday soon that would change, so I soaked up memories of now to keep me sane for that day.

"Good jumping, Milo," Sydney said as he raced past us to the playroom. She chuckled when he bumped into the door-frame, not slowing down enough to make the turn.

Her eyes met mine, and her smile wavered as she glanced away. Was she nervous?

"Do you want a turn?" she asked.

I laughed. "No, I'm good being a judge."

"You just don't want your butt kicked by four-year-olds."

"My ego isn't that big. I know they're faster than me. I'm not sure how much crawling and jumping my body can tolerate."

She smirked. "You make it sound like you're seventy."

I shrugged. "Sometimes it feels like it. Hockey isn't exactly easy on the body."

"You seem to be holding up just fine." Her eyes ran the length of my arms, and I fought the urge to flex. Was she flirting or just making an observation? It had been way, way too long for me to be able to tell the difference.

Her checking me out was one thing. Hard to miss, but easily excusable. I was well aware of my athletic build. It was my job to be in top physical condition. I'd been on the cover of men's magazines with headlines boasting about my training routine and diet. People staring at my body became a norm before I even joined the league.

It was the words I didn't know how to decipher.

I didn't know how to respond, and with each passing second the voice in my mind screaming *loser* got louder.

As much as I wanted to play cool and aloof, I knew I wasn't. "Are you flirting?"

Her eyes widened, and her cheeks instantly reddened. "I... um..."

I smiled, pleased I managed to throw her off like she did to me. "I mean that as a genuine question. It's been so long since I've been single or noticed a woman who isn't my ex, I really don't know."

"Done!" Milo jumped out of the room and landed on all fours in front of Sydney. She held up her hand and gave him a high five.

"That was your fastest one yet! Five minutes and twenty-six seconds."

"Good job!" Finn celebrated with Milo before rushing toward their room. "I want to go again!"

"Yell 'go' for me," Sydney called after him.

We waited in a charged silence until Finn shouted. She got lucky with the interruption, but I wasn't letting her off the hook.

"So? Were you?"

She rubbed her hand over her cheek and cringed. "I guess I was."

"Don't be embarrassed. I don't mind." I winked, and she ducked her head. "I just didn't know. I also don't know how to reply."

She suddenly burst out laughing. "You really are an old man."

I shot her a playful glare before joining in. "You're right. I am."

The tension between us disappeared, and we went back to cheering on Finn as he ran through the hall to the playroom.

She made one flirtatious comment. That didn't have to mean anything. She could have been joking. I hated that I knew exactly who could help me with this, but admitting it to them wasn't worth it.

The guys would never, ever, for the rest of my life let me live it down.

I was on my own to navigate this strange, new world.

The next day we had a short practice schedule, so I was able to stay and play with the boys for almost an hour before leaving for the arena. What that really meant was I had an hour to overthink every single thing Sydney said or did.

She admitted to flirting with me once. That meant it could happen again. I had to get better at figuring it out.

Unless it really was a one-time thing, and I embarrassed her so much that she would never dare do it again. That was a worst case scenario. I liked the playfulness we'd developed. It was effortless, until I started overthinking everything.

"Where's your head, Dad?" Reese smacked his stick on the ice, drawing my attention. "Come on, you should have had that pass."

I ignored him and waited for my turn to come again. We were running drills, and I let my body go on autopilot while I thought about Sydney. Not the time. I shook my head and focused on leading the guys.

An hour later, Coach called it, and I headed to the bench to get a drink.

Chloe was waiting for us. She'd been doing that a lot lately. She gave updates to some of us, pointers to the rookies, and then she waved me down.

I hated that she always made me wait until the end. The

anticipation never helped with the blow that was sure to come.

"Hey, Dad." She waited for me to sit next to her, and I knew it was bad today.

"What's going on?"

"The wicked witch has been hard at work." She paused and met my eyes. "Sorry, I shouldn't call her that. She's still the boys' mom."

I sighed. "Trust me, I call her a lot worse in my mind."

She smiled, but it didn't last long. "She took the opportunity just like we knew she would. More and more 'sources close to the couple' are backing up her story about you and Sydney. They're making you out to be an adulterer and terrible father."

Per my request, Chloe hadn't gotten involved. Despite her desperation to get back at Olivia for what she was doing. It was like dangling a steak in front of a rabid wolf. She wanted to tear her limb from limb. She didn't tolerate people hurting her family, and the boys and I were a part of that. I knew the moment I gave her the go ahead, she would have emails sent and calls made.

I wasn't there yet. I didn't want to add fuel to the inferno. I didn't want to give the reporters anything. One word or reaction would last them days. They could write article after article of garbage analyzing that one action.

I didn't want to give them anything.

"What is it going to take for this to just go away?" I asked, mostly to myself.

"She's a leech. She's going to milk this attention for all it's worth. Right now, she's getting more sympathy than she ever did through the divorce. Now that she's not the bad guy, she's in heaven. She can pretend to be the heartbroken woman scorned. She's able to spin her reasoning for not wanting custody of the boys. She's blaming you for all her emotional trauma. How she had to get far away and work on herself so she could live her best life and eventually be a better mother."

I scoffed. "Yeah, that's what she's doing."

"I know the truth. You do. The team does. I know you don't care, but at some point this is all going to start hurting you. You want it to disappear, but I don't think that's going to happen anytime soon. She's already drug it out another week. You can't risk losing sponsorship and endorsements over this. Don't let her do that to you. She's taken enough."

She was right. The bad press hadn't affected me too much yet. The companies I worked with knew me well enough to let it slide. But if Olivia kept this up, kept spinning stories, I might not walk out of this without losing something.

I slumped down, resting my elbows on my knees. "So? What do you suggest?"

"We need to get aggressive. Your attorney needs to issue a threat for defamation. Your agent needs to contact your current contracts and make sure they know this is all a bunch of garbage." She paused. "I also think you need to issue your own statement, explaining that Sydney is the boys' nanny, you've only known her for a few weeks, and that there is nothing romantic going on between you."

I flinched, and of course she caught it.

"Unless there is something there?" Just like that, she switched from vicious business woman to overinvolved friend.

"There isn't something *not* there. I don't know." I couldn't even figure out flirting. How was I supposed to know if she had more feelings for me than just professional or friendship?

"Then we'll just skip that part." She made the decision for me.

"It won't make things worse?"

She shook her head. "There's no way of knowing for sure until we try."

I didn't see any other options. We had to end this before it got out of control.

"Okay. I'll do it."

"Perfect. I'll make the calls." She stood and walked away while I stared at the ice.

12

SYDNEY

B randon was acting strange. He came home from practice and immediately went to his room to pack. The boys didn't seem to notice anything off, but I could see it in his face. What happened today? I wanted to find him and ask, but that wasn't my responsibility. I was here for the boys.

"Do you guys want to make your Dad a card? We'll tell him to read it on the plane." I hoped that would cheer him up and take him out of whatever funk he was in.

"Yeah!" they cheered in perfect unison. I smiled and led them up to their playroom where they had a coloring table. Sometimes I wondered if they rehearsed their synchronization or if it was just a twin thing.

I got out a stack of colored paper and fanned it out so they could pick. "We'll each make one so he has lots to read."

They got excited about that, and Milo picked red while Finn picked green. I took a yellow paper and set out the box of markers and stickers so they could decorate them.

Milo folded his in half, almost, and handed it to me. "Can you write for me?"

"Of course." I took the card and waited. "What do you want it to say?"

"I want 'Go Fury' on the outside and 'I love you' on the inside." He handed me a purple marker and pointed. "Use this color."

It took a lot of effort not to tear up. He was so sweet. He knew exactly what his dad would need to hear. "Do you want bubble letters so you can color them in?"

He smiled and bobbed his head repeatedly. "Yeah!"

I did my best, struggling to remember how to make each letter. It had been years, if not more than a decade since I last did this, but it seemed like a good idea when I thought of it. The *Y*'s were a little funky, but it was a decent effort.

"There you go. I left room so you can sign the bottom. Do you want me to help you?" The boys were getting better at writing their names, but I still wanted to offer.

He opened the card and picked up a blue marker. With slow, purposeful strokes, he made a capital *M* then hesitated.

"*I*," Finn told him calmly.

Milo drew the next letter then the *L* on his own. His eyes met mine, and his tongue was peeking out of his mouth, his sign of concentration.

"Good job! One more letter."

He stared down and said his name slowly before drawing a large *O*.

"Perfect!" I held up my hand and he high-fived me with pride on his face.

He shuffled through the sticker box while Finn happily scribbled on the front of his card.

"What are you drawing?" I asked

"The arena. Here's the ice and the puck and the people and there's Dad." He pointed at a block figure.

"That's great. He's going to love it."

"Will you write for me too?" He didn't take a break from his drawing.

"Yeah, when you're done I'll write whatever you want."

While I was waiting for him, I made my card, writing 'Good Luck' on the front. I drew a stack of pancakes on the inside and said if they won their games, we'd have a pancake party when he got back. It was cheesy, but a construction paper card didn't really call for deep thoughts.

I added a few silly stickers and then got up to look around for an envelope or a way to wrap them so it would be a surprise. There were probably proper envelopes in his office, but I didn't feel right going in there. I took two pieces of black paper and taped them together so we could drop our cards in there and he couldn't see through.

"I'm done," Milo called and handed me his card. I smiled at the mismatched letters of blue, pink, green, and every other color he could find.

"He's going to love it."

I sat next to Finn while Milo went off to play with cars on the course we designed.

"Can you help me with my name?" Finn asked in a small voice.

"Sure." He opened the card and poised his marker right in the center. I didn't correct him. I loved seeing what they did naturally. "Okay, do you know the first letter?"

He nodded and drew a lower-case *f* then immediately drew the *i*. "We both have *I*'s second."

I smiled. "You're right. Good job."

He paused and looked up at me. "I need help."

"*N* is next."

He nodded, but didn't write it. "Can you show me?"

I pulled a piece of paper toward me and drew a lower-case *n*. His brows scrunched together.

"That's not what my teacher's look like."

Huh. Maybe she showed him the uppercase version? I drew that one and he perked up. "Yeah! That. Sometimes I do it wrong."

"Here, you can trace mine a few times, then write it on the card."

I slid the paper to him, and he carefully drew over my letter twice before pushing it out of the way. He wrote two perfect *N*'s on the card then looked up at me.

"That's it. You did it!"

His smile took over his face. "Yay!"

"Do you want to write anything on the inside?"

He tapped his marker on the table. "Go Daddy and Olli."

I had to bite my lip to keep from smiling. I loved that he had a favorite player already. He probably liked him from knowing him in the real world, but it was still cute. I was sure Olli would be happy when he found out.

"Do you want bubble letters like Milo's so you can color them in?"

He shook his head. "I want to put stickers on."

I wrote out his request and then passed it back. "All set for you."

"Thanks." He loaded the card with every variety of sticker, then leaned back. "All done."

"It looks so good. He's going to love it."

He smiled and went to meet Milo on the carpet. I put the cards in the makeshift envelope and taped it shut.

I got down to play with them and several minutes passed before Brandon walked in.

"Hey, guys. What are you doing?"

They jumped up and ran to give him hugs.

"We're playing race cars," Milo replied. I was worried for a moment they would share our secret, but they seemed to have moved on already.

"Great. Sydney, can I talk to you for a second?" He didn't seem as stressed as before, which was a good sign. I stood and followed him down the hall while the boys went back to playing.

"What's up?" I asked, hoping this wasn't a serious conversation.

"I didn't mention this before, but while I'm away you'll sleep in the guestroom so you're closer to the boys."

"Yeah, like I did last time." It wasn't like I was going to let them sleep in this huge house by themselves.

"Right, of course. Sorry, my head is in a million places. I should have assumed you were more on top of things than me." The worry had returned, wrinkling his forehead.

"Is everything okay?"

He sighed, dropping his shoulders. "I hope so."

Well that was ominous. "Anything I should know about?"

It wasn't my place or my business to pry, but I couldn't help it. His body language screamed that something was off.

"There have been pictures of you and the boys from the game going around the internet."

I huffed out a laugh. "Why?"

His eyes met mine. "There are rumors that you're my new girlfriend."

My heart should not have skipped at the idea of that being true.

I'd convinced myself that no one but the people right around us at the game ever even noticed me. I was wrong, apparently.

"Did you set them straight?"

He nodded. "Chloe's been working on it." He hesitated. "That's not all of it."

"Okay? What else?" He was opening up to me, which was great. I wanted to relieve any of the burden I could. Anything to take the strain away.

"Chloe stopped me after practice today. The rumors have gotten out of control. The worst case scenario we came up with a few days ago has come true. Tabloids are saying I had an affair with you, and that's what broke up my marriage."

I didn't know if I should laugh or scream. "Are you kidding me? I've been here for a few weeks."

"I know." He sighed.

"I mean, in Utah." I let out a humorless laugh. "There's plenty of proof of that. I don't have any social media accounts, but my friends in Denver did. They could tell anyone who asked that I was there."

"Chloe's already working on that, too. I'm sure she'll get it all shut down soon, but I just wanted to let you know."

This was why he looked like there was a two ton boulder on his shoulders. Me. It wasn't my fault, I knew that, but I still felt bad.

"I'm so sorry, Brandon."

His eyes flashed to mine. "Don't apologize. You did nothing wrong. You've been nothing but amazing."

He paused and took a half step closer to me. I scanned his face, pausing at his lips. He was close enough. If either of us moved...

"I'll do everything I can to get this under control quickly, but just be aware that there's a chance the press might be interested in you."

That got my attention, and I narrowed my eyes. "What does that mean?"

"If they get a hold of your phone number somehow, they'll call. Hopefully they don't come here for pictures, but it's a possibility."

I nearly choked. I was a nobody from central Pennsylvania. I was a nanny, not some celebrity.

"Should I be nervous?"

He shook his head. "No. Maybe just hang out at home tomorrow with the boys after school."

"Got it."

"Thanks, Sydney." He reached out and squeezed my wrist.

There it was. He made the move. Closed the gap. I tilted

my head up, and we locked eyes. The energy between us changed. He lowered his head as I sucked in a breath.

"Daddy! Come see!" Milo yelled as he ran toward us.

We both jumped back and Brandon gave me one last smile before walking back to the playroom.

I went down to the pool house in a daze. I mindlessly packed the essentials so I could stay in the main house without having to run back and forth.

He might have been able to distract me, but I still saw it. Brandon was downplaying everything. I could tell. He probably didn't want to scare me, but him holding back was worse than telling me everything. I'd just be the most boring person in the world, and hopefully the press would lose interest. The boys would be fine playing at home for one or two days, but I wasn't sure how long I could say no to their requests to go to different parks or the museum. It wasn't like I could tell them anything. I'd just have to get creative.

T he boys were full of energy when I picked them up from school. They ran in front of me to the car and then ran back to me before returning. What had their teacher given them?

"Did you guys have a good day?"

"Yeah!" Milo thrust his fist in the air while his brother nodded aggressively next to him.

"What did you do?" I made sure they were both buckled before getting in.

"We made rock candy," Finn replied, and I nearly pounded my head against the headrest. Of course they did.

"Yeah, Ms. Stephanie gave us a string, and then we watched it make colored rocks." Milo confirmed my fear.

"Then you ate it?" It wasn't so much a question as it was me resigning to how the rest of the day was going to go. I needed something active for them to do to burn off this energy.

"Yeah!" they shouted with unnecessary volume. Wonderful.

On the drive back to the house, I ran through a list of possibilities. They liked the playset in the backyard, but their interest only lasted about a half hour or so. I might be able to stretch it to an hour if I came up with games for them to play on it. It wasn't enough. The pool was the next best option.

"Do you guys want to swim today?"

"Yeah!" This one was twice as loud as the last. At least they liked the idea. Hopefully I wasn't setting myself up for an epic breakdown once the sugar high ended.

As we pulled in, I told them to get changed while I called for backup. It was an abnormally warm day, so maybe I could bring in someone else.

"Hey Sydney," Emma answered.

"Hi, how's it going?"

"Good?" She dragged out the word. "What's going on?"

"The boys and I are getting in the pool, and I was wondering if you and Jackson wanted to join us."

"Huh, that sounds fun."

"Oh good." I didn't mean to sound as desperate as I was, but I was distracted by what Brandon told me, the almost kiss, and now the boys were next-level crazy.

"We'll be over in a few minutes."

"Great, see you soon."

I hung up and ran to the pool house to change into a suit before hunting down the boys. Milo wore his Spiderman swim trunks, but Finn was staring at a pile of clothes with a pout bordering on tears.

"What's wrong?" I knelt down next to him.

"I can't find my Iron Man shorts."

"Okay, we'll look for them." I rifled through the pile, then pulled a box from his closet marked 'Summer Clothes.' I found three pairs of trunks, but he shook his head at each one.

"Mommy always knew where they were." His dejection nearly broke my heart. This was the first time he'd mentioned her around me, and I wasn't sure what to say. She should be here. She should be getting ready to play with them.

What woman could walk away from her kids? Especially when they were so sweet and loving? It made me furious.

I was about to dump the box on the ground in defeat when I saw a red mask. "Ah ha!" I pulled them out and held the shorts up for Finn to see.

"You found them!"

I tossed them over and began putting things away while he changed.

"Ready?" Milo bounced on his toes near the door.

"Yeah!" Finn shouted as they took off running.

I dropped the pile of clothes and hurried after them.

"We need sunscreen before we go out," I called as they reached the bottom of the stairs.

Sunscreen, water, towels, floaties. I repeated it over and over until I completed each step. We just made it to the pool and the boys jumped in when I heard voices. I spun to see Emma walking up with Jackson on her hip and a woman with a blond bob next to her with a baby sitting happily on her shoulders. I vaguely recognized her from the game, but I couldn't remember her name.

"Sydney!" Emma waved and the boys hurried out of the pool to greet the guests.

"Hi Emma! Hi Addi." Their attention quickly moved on to the babies, reaching up and talking to them.

"Hi guys." I helped take Emma's oversized beach bag and sat it next to the row of lounge chairs.

"This is Addison, I think you guys met at the game, but there was a lot going on."

Addison smiled at me while lowering her baby to her lap. "I hope you don't mind. Today's my day off so Emma invited me along."

"Not at all. The more the merrier." I smiled at her little boy who ducked his face into her neck.

"This is Eli. He'll warm up to you in a few minutes." She spread out her towel and sat him on it before grabbing a bottle of sunscreen from the bag.

"Thanks so much for coming. The boys made rock candy at school and I needed a way to burn off as much energy as possible."

"Oh! That's just mean," Emma said with a laugh.

Milo and Finn ran past us to the slide, and I shook my head. "Slow down, guys. I don't want you to slip."

They actually listened and walked the rest of the way. Huh. I hadn't expected that to work so easily.

"I'm impressed," Addison said with a nod.

Once their babies were lathered in sunscreen, we climbed into the shallow end and watched the twins play. It was nice having some company, and it was a good distraction from the worries on my mind.

I almost forgot we were under house arrest.

13

BRANDON

We won against the Phoenix team, but we were playing San Diego tonight and they were right behind us in the division rankings. They were going to make us work for each point, but I knew the guys wanted it. We'd been working too hard, putting in too much time to let any team get in our heads. It was at the point in the season where each win was important. We only had a three-point lead over them in our division, and getting the two points from a win would make that gap much more comfortable as we cemented ourselves for the playoffs.

I had a few minutes before I had to head down to meet with the press, so I called Sydney hoping I could talk with the boys.

She answered, and we switched it over to a video call. I took in her bright eyes and smile and felt more relaxed. She had a calming effect on me. Well, except my heart; that always started to race when I saw her. "Hey, you look fancy."

I looked down at my maroon suit and gave her my best model look. "Why, thank you."

She giggled and shook her head. It was the best sound in

the world. I couldn't remember the last time someone made me feel this happy and light. It had been a long, long time.

"Congrats on the win last night. I'd say it was a good game, but it didn't seem like it was all that hard for you guys. Milo said the team didn't even show up. I'm assuming that's something he picked up from you?"

I chuckled. "Announcers say that all the time, too. It's not just me trash talking."

"Uh huh." She walked through the house until I recognized the playroom. "Guys, your dad's on the phone."

They both dropped the Legos they were building and rushed to sit on either side of her.

"Hi Dad!" Milo waved.

"Daddy, did you get our cards?" Finn asked.

"Yeah, thank you so much. Those made me so happy." It was the sweetest thing, opening them on the plane. They'd never done anything like that for me before Sydney came, and I'd never admit it out loud, but it made me tear up a bit. "Olli said thank you too."

Finn beamed and whispered something to Sydney. She nodded and he faced me. "We swam in the pool yesterday with Eli and Jackson, and guess what, Dad!"

"What?"

"I swam all the way across the pool without my floaties!" he boasted.

"Whoa! Great job." I couldn't believe I missed that. It was disappointing, but a cost of the job. I was just grateful they trusted Sydney enough to take risks.

Sydney smiled down at him with the same pride I felt. "I was right there next to him, but he was so brave."

"That's amazing. They had swim lessons last summer and learned to swim on their own, but they wanted to keep their floaties anyway."

"And I went down the big slide by myself!" Milo added, not wanting to be left out.

"You did?" He normally asked me or at least Finn to go with him. He was pretty fearless, but every time he got to the top of that slide, he froze.

"Yeah." He seemed to puff out his chest. "Sydney said we should get swim trunks with our faces on them since we're superheroes now too."

I laughed as Sydney looked down at him with what I was pretty sure was love in her eyes. The boys managed to worm their way into her heart. I shouldn't have been too surprised. They were pretty good at winning people over. I couldn't help but feel a tiny bit jealous though. It was amazing how much she cared about them, and as a father that was an incredible blessing. I just wished she lit up like that when she saw me.

"Are you being good for Sydney?"

They both nodded.

"Thank you. I miss you guys."

"I miss you too, Daddy," Milo said.

"Love you, Daddy." Finn smiled once more at me before disappearing. Milo followed, and Sydney sighed.

"Sorry. Legos win."

"They are a lot more interesting than me."

She smiled, and it made the edges of her eyes crinkle. I wanted to trace the lines with my fingers.

Whoa. I shook that thought away.

"I don't think so," she teased.

"Well, at least one person at home still cares about me." I smiled. I was pretty sure this was flirting.

She tilted her head, making her honey-colored hair fall over her shoulder like a waterfall. "There's at least two of us at any point in time."

I chuckled. "Well, thanks. That makes me feel a lot better."

"I try. So I invited Emma over, and Addison came too. I really like them. I hope you don't mind."

Both women had already texted me, telling me how much

they loved Sydney and the way she was with the boys. They were both very much Team Sydney and warned me not to screw it up.

"I don't mind at all. I'm glad you're making friends."

"Me too." Her gaze dropped. "It's been a really long time since I've had anyone I really cared about. Even longer since I felt at home somewhere."

But she felt that at my home? My heart swelled, but I felt guilty. "How long has it been since you went home?"

"Ten years. I had a fight with my parents and they told me I was no longer welcome."

"I'm so sorry." I couldn't imagine not seeing or speaking to my own family for that long. We weren't necessarily close, but I always knew they were there for me if I needed them.

"It's for the best." She tried to smile, but I could tell it still hurt her.

"Well, we care about you. The boys..." I hesitated to use the L-word, but it was true. I could see it. "They really like you. They don't take to everyone the way they have to you. That means so much to me."

"Me too." Finally, a genuine grin appeared. "And the way everyone has welcomed me and made sure I was included." She shook her head. "I never expected that. Thank you, Brandon."

There was a lot left unsaid, but I just smiled. "Thank you, Sydney."

She turned and shook her head with a laugh. "They're making quite the mess. I'd better stop them before every block they own is on the floor. Good luck tonight. We'll be watching."

"Thanks." I paused. "Oh, and Syd?"

She raised her brows. "Yes?"

"Don't think I forgot about our interruption. We'll be revisiting that when I get back."

There. That was me being forward. Letting her know I was interested.

She bit her lip while her smile grew. "Bye, Brandon."

"Bye, Syd."

She might have started out as a nanny, someone to be there for the boys, but at some point things changed. She was so much more than that. She was a part of our family. She was a friend and confidante for me. If we got to this point so quickly, what would the future bring? Was there hope for more?

I felt incredible now. Invincible. I had my boys and one of the most amazing women I'd ever known cheering me on. This was the fire I needed to help get the team going. Tonight was going to be great.

———

We got to the arena and were led to where the press was set up.

"Hartman, Cullen, Schultz, Malkin at table one." A younger guy with a headset pointed to the closest long table.

We headed over, but Chloe appeared and cut us off, staring directly at me. "I need to talk to you."

"What's going on?" Hartman asked with a stern expression.

She gave me a meaningful look, but I didn't move. "It's okay. You can tell them. They're going to find out when the questions start anyway."

"I tried to kill the story before it took off, but Olivia spoke to the tabloids. Again. She's adamant that Sydney is the cause of your divorce."

I pinched the bridge of my nose while Erik laughed. "How can she claim that? Sydney's only been here for like a month."

Chloe shot her brother a sharp look. "Because she's addicted to attention. That's not all, Brandon."

She wasn't calling me Dad or Cullen. This was serious. "What else?"

Was there anything else she could say to make this worse?

"She's saying she's pregnant."

I burst out laughing. "Well, tell her congratulations."

Chloe looked at me like I'd just grown a second head. "It's not funny. She's claiming it's yours, and you've abandoned her."

"We haven't lived in the same house in eight months, and before that it wasn't like we were intimate. If she is actually pregnant, it's not mine."

"Well, the rest of the world doesn't know that. Your divorce has only been official for three months. That's right along with her timeframe."

"Good thing we're around him every day and know his personal life. We can set things straight," Noah said with confidence.

Chloe sighed. "I don't know how much weight that will carry. You're his teammates. Of course you'll have his back."

"Maybe if they interview them while we're doing ours," Hartman pointed to some of our other teammates. "No one else knows what's going on, so they'll get genuine reactions."

She seemed to consider it. "I'll try to steer the reporters in that direction."

"I should just call her." That was the last thing I wanted to do, especially right before a big game, but I didn't see a better option.

"Don't. That could just make things worse. Let's try dealing with it from our side for now." Chloe was the one who knew what she was doing, so I agreed.

"Thanks for the heads up, Chloe." I really did appreciate all the effort she was putting into helping me, but I knew it was driving her crazy not having control over the situation.

We moved toward the table and sat in front of the microphones that were already set up. The guys were tense, and I hated that my personal drama was affecting them. I couldn't let this continue onto the ice.

"You have ten minutes," the guy with the headset announced to the reporters in front of us.

The questions started out pretty routine. How did we feel about the Phoenix game? Were we ready to take on San Diego? The same things we were asked before every game.

"Three minutes!" our moderator shouted.

"Cullen, what do you have to say about the affair?"

I fought the urge to roll my eyes. "There was no affair. The woman in question has been the nanny for my sons for a month. We never met before that."

I tried to keep the information as limited as possible, and I didn't want to say Sydney's name. Anything to keep the attention off of her.

"Your ex is claiming the nanny is the reason for your separation," another voice shouted.

"What does this have to do with the game or the team?" Hartman asked with venom in his voice.

That made the group quiet for about five seconds. "Your ex is saying she's pregnant with your child, and that you're denying it's yours so you can continue your relationship with Sydney Banks."

Of course, she was.

Wait. They found her full name? That wasn't a good sign.

"My ex and I have been separated for over eight months, which is the time that she moved to LA. I'm sure you guys can do the math."

"That's it." Headset guy stood in front of us and told us to move on to the next table.

"You don't have to. Just head into the locker room," Hartman said.

I knew the coaches and front office would be understanding if I skipped out, but I didn't want to do anything to fuel the rumors. "No, I've got to show them it doesn't bother me."

"It's bothering me," Erik said. "Olivia was a witch while you were married, and I thought you'd escaped her, but turns out she can still get her claws wrapped around you."

"I appreciate the support, guys. Let's just try to keep them focused on the game," I said as we sat down.

Erik and Noah shared a smile, and I knew I'd just created a game for them. This group of reporters didn't spend even five minutes on questions about the game or the team before setting in on a personal attack. I sat back while my friends took over.

"Are you denying you're having another child with your ex?" a voice called out.

Noah leaned forward. "As a team, we've been focused on improving our game this year to make sure we make it to the playoffs. Together we took a vow of celibacy after winning the cup last year."

Erik smirked. His wife and sister were both pregnant at the moment, so that was sure to cause some problems if the reporters took their attention off me for even half a second.

"Sydney Banks lives at your house, how can you prove that you didn't have an affair?"

"I would think that such fine, dedicated journalists such as yourselves would be able to put it together, but the only person Brandon has ever had an affair with was me!" Erik said with as much passion as a soap opera actress. He put his hand up to his forehead and pretended to faint into the chair.

Hartman stood up from his chair and slapped me on the back of the head. "Not him too? Cullen! I thought what we shared was something special!" He threw his head back and stormed off.

Noah was chuckling but composed himself. "And I thought you said it was only me!"

He covered his face with both hands and made sobbing sounds.

We would hear about this later when the coaches and management saw this playback, but I didn't really care. The reporters were stunned into silence, but a few had smiles and were shaking their heads. At least they realized how ridiculous they were being.

I was grateful for teammates who had my back. It was better going into a game laughing together than burdened with drama we could do nothing about.

14

SYDNEY

"**A**re you sure there isn't anything I can do to help?" I asked Brandon for the second time.

His ex was out of her mind, claiming she was pregnant with his baby. How would that even be possible? She'd been gone for months.

"No, I just wanted to talk to you."

I smiled, happy he thought of calling me when he needed someone.

"I know it doesn't feel like it, but one day this will all be behind you."

He sighed. "I can't wait."

"At least you guys won." I tried to cheer him up. He sounded so upset.

"Yeah, we kind of had to after the stunts we pulled with the press. Coach threatened to bench all of us if we didn't pull off a win."

The women sent me clips of the guys being completely absurd the night before. I didn't want to think about how the coaches reacted to that.

"Tell them I enjoyed their performance."

"I will." He chuckled. "I can't wait to get back home."

"Me too." I cringed. "I mean the boys are excited."

"It's okay for you to be excited too."

I covered my face even though he couldn't see me blushing. "I didn't say that."

"You didn't have to." He countered.

I laughed and waved to the boys as they ran past me to the car. "The dynamic duo is out."

I held out the phone and put it on speaker. "It's your dad."

"Hi Daddy!" they shouted.

"Hey, guys."

"Snow cone time!" Finn cheered, and then Milo repeated it until they were chanting the three words.

"I'd better go before they stage a coup."

"Okay, have fun. I'll see you guys tomorrow." He laughed and hung up.

The boys were practically vibrating with excitement as we pulled away from the preschool. I'd seen a few snow cone stands open for the season and said that if they were super good last night and today at school, we could get one this afternoon.

It was the only thing they talked about since I brought it up.

"I want blue," Finn announced.

"I want red and pink." Milo rushed out as if he might not get his choice if he didn't tell me now.

"Sounds good." I'd have to figure out what flavors those colors meant when we got there. I turned onto the street and headed toward the closest stand I remembered seeing. This distraction was as much for me as it was for the boys. After Brandon called yesterday and told me that the worst case scenario had happened, that the press picked up the story about me being his mistress and they knew my full name. I had to do something to keep my mind off things.

We made him a welcome home sign last night while the boys told me all of their snow cone experiences. I tried to give them my full attention, but my mind kept wandering. How had they gotten my last name? In the quiet of the night, after the boys were asleep, I wondered if someone in the Pride told them but quickly dismissed it. The Pride and the team were Brandon's family.

Maybe his ex knew? Did she ask when he hired me?

I was up all night worrying. Brandon said the press might be interested in me, but so far things had been quiet. We stayed at home and only ventured out for school. That was why I thought a treat would be a good idea. The boys were getting restless and deserved something to look forward to.

"I want one this big." Finn held up his hands to frame his face.

I laughed and agreed as I got in the left turn lane. A gray sedan pulled behind me. I noticed it when I pulled out of the preschool. It had been going the same way, turn for turn.

Once was random. Twice was a coincidence. Three times was intentional.

I read that last night. I wanted to be prepared in case there were cameras following us. I read to make four right turns if you were in a city to see if they followed. We were already past four turns now. I took the next right turn and they followed. This was definitely intentional.

How could I call the police without scaring the boys? I turned up their favorite music and faded it to play just in the backseat. They seemed happy to sing along so I pulled out my phone and called nine-one-one.

"Nine-one-one, what's your emergency," a woman answered

"I think I'm being followed in my car." I tried to keep my voice as normal as possible. I told them about taking random turns and that it was likely a paparazzi.

"Can you get to the police station?"

That was another fact I'd memorized when I couldn't

sleep. We were quite far from it. "I can, but it's about ten minutes away."

"Head that direction. I'll send an officer your way as well."

I kept an eye on the car while I turned onto the road that headed straight to the station. I just had to get to the other side of downtown now. A red car turned out from another street and got behind me. I relaxed for a second thinking the gray car might get stuck at a light, but then I saw a camera appear out of the passenger window.

"There's another car. They've got a camera sticking out of their window."

"Try not to panic, ma'am. There's an officer heading in your direction."

"Okay." There wasn't anything else I could do. I drove the speed limit, staying in my lane, and hoped they would get bored and leave us alone.

"I have two four-year-olds with me," I felt the need to mention, hoping it might get the officer here sooner.

"I understand. I've notified the officers so they are aware."

"Thank you." We were halfway there. If only the lights would work in my favor. I hated having to stop, knowing they were able to get closer to us.

The light went green and I drove, nearly making it to the other side of the intersection when I noticed a car turn out, cutting off the red car behind me. Their wheels screeched and dread washed over me.

"There's a third car now. A blue SUV."

"The officer is about two minutes away."

I swallowed and tightened my grip on the wheel. That was too far away. The station was even farther than that, though. I had no choice but to keep going. I checked on the boys and they were singing and laughing at each other. Good. The last thing I wanted was for them to be scared.

A black car seemed to appear out of nowhere, a huge

camera aimed at us, as it cut off the SUV. I nearly cried out when it almost hit us.

"There's another one. A black car." My heart was racing and it took everything in me not to panic. I wanted to pull over and wait for the police to catch up, but that would give these predators more opportunity.

"Ma'am, try to remain calm. The officer is at nine hundred south. He should be able to intercept in a moment."

That was only a block behind me, but the light had just turned red. If he didn't go through with his lights and siren, we were just getting farther away.

I watched in my rearview mirror as the four cars grew more aggressive, swerving back and forth across the lanes to block each other. I relayed that to the operator. "They're getting closer and closer to my car."

The light turned yellow in front of me and I accelerated, hoping to lose them. The light went red, but they all came through the intersection with me.

"You're close to the station now. Just remain calm."

"I can see it. Just a couple more lights."

We were almost there. So close. I tightened my grip and sighed when the next light turned green so I didn't have to stop. I checked again, and the cars were still cutting each other off.

"Sydney!" Milo screamed behind me. I looked to my right and saw a white SUV heading straight for us with another camera out. I slammed on the brakes just in time for it to crash into me.

---

a'am, can you hear me?" Light flashed in my eyes for a split second, then darkness.
"Normal dilation."

Something tightened around my neck, but I couldn't move. My entire body hurt in a way I'd never felt before.

What happened?

I heard crying, and somewhere deep in my mind I knew I should be concerned. Who was crying?

"Finn?" I tried to speak, but it came out like a wheeze.

"We have the boys," a voice said near me. I tried to open my eyes, but it was impossible.

The crying continued. Milo was asking for me. I could hear his little voice wobble. I needed to go to him. Tell him everything was okay.

"Ma'am, we need you to relax. You were in an accident."

"Boys," I croaked out.

"They're okay. Just a scrape on one and possibly whiplash with the other. They're going to be just fine."

That's what I needed to know. "Brandon."

"Who's Brandon?"

"Call Brandon." I was barely able to get the words out before the pain took over and everything faded to black.

15

BRANDON

My agent was not amused by our press conference. "You can't give them anything, Cullen. Nothing. You guys might have thought you were being funny, but mark my word, tomorrow there will be even more rumors. They're going to say the entire team is a part of some twisted relationship thing."

I highly doubted that. "Sorry, Ben, but we were all sick of the same questions. They have no information, so they're just digging."

"And listening to Olivia. I already had your attorney reach out and threaten a stack of lawsuits if she doesn't stop."

Yeah, that wasn't likely to help. She didn't care about the consequences; she was too high on the attention right now.

"What do you want me to do?"

"Shut up. That's what I want. Repeat after me, 'No comment.' Can you do that?" Ben wasn't normally one to lose his cool, so I decided not to poke the bear.

"Fine. I can do that."

"Good. Just lay low until you get home. Don't leave the hotel."

"I wasn't planning on it."

"Make sure Sydney stays in too. The boys might have to miss a day or two of school, but the sooner the paps realize they can't get anything, the sooner they'll move on."

"You really think they'll give up?"

"As soon as someone more famous does something more scandalous they'll forget all about you."

"That's all I could ever want." I wasn't normally one to wish ill on someone else, but come on. Why was Hollywood suddenly on good behavior?

"I'm working with Chloe to make this all go away, but for now, make our lives as easy as possible."

"Got it." I hung up and tossed my phone on the bed. We were flying out in about six hours, so it wasn't like I'd have to be on lockdown for long.

There was a knock on my door and when I opened it, Reese, Hartman, and Olli pushed past me.

"Come on in." I shook my head and closed the door behind them.

"Chloe said you're grounded, so we're here to keep you company."

"Thanks. Not in the mood for Sea World?" I asked with a smirk. San Diego was a fun city to have a few extra hours in, but with how often we were here, it lost some of the excitement. The younger guys still loved exploring and hitting up the main attractions, though.

"Nah." Olli dropped down on my bed and kicked his feet up.

"We were thinking of ordering in and just relaxing," Hartman said.

"Sounds good." I settled on the couch next to Reese while Hartman jumped onto the other side of the bed.

Olli found an old action movie, but it was a weak attempt at distraction.

"Is she worth all this?" Reese asked out of nowhere.

"Who?" I replied.

He shifted to face me. "Sydney. You haven't known her for that long. Wouldn't it be easier to just find a new nanny? It wouldn't get rid of all the rumors, but it would help."

Was he insane? "I'm not just going to fire her for something she had nothing to do with."

"It would make it easier if she was out of the picture," Olli said with a shrug.

"Where is this coming from? You guys have met her. You all like her." I was stunned they were saying this.

"We just don't want you involved with another woman who causes drama and heartache for you. You barely survived Olivia. You don't need to go through something like that again," Hartman said in what I assumed he thought was a diplomatic manner.

"I can't believe you guys. I've supported each of you. Olli, when you had your accident and turned into a monster, I was there. Reese, I welcomed you onto the team and made sure you didn't give up on Chloe." I turned to my captain. "And you. I've been on this team for thirteen years. I've supported you and stood up for you through it all. How can you guys not have the same respect for me now?"

I was generally a pretty calm person, but my blood was boiling.

The three of them shared a look. Another knock sounded and Olli got up and brought in bags of food. He set them on the table and started unloading like I hadn't just lost my temper.

"Seriously, guys?" I shouted.

Reese smirked, and I nearly punched it off his face. "We were just checking."

"He's in love," Olli called from the other side of the suite.

"I knew it," Hartman said. He stood and clapped me on the shoulder as he passed.

"What? What are you guys talking about?"

"We just wanted to make sure you were serious about this girl," Olli said with a shrug.

"And we wanted to see if *you* knew how you felt about her." Reese relaxed against the couch, looking much too cocky.

"So that was some twisted reverse psychology crap?" I got to my feet and paced.

"It worked, didn't it?" Hartman asked.

Well, they certainly got a reaction out of me. Of course, my first instinct was to defend and protect Sydney. She was amazing and selfless and had done nothing to deserve the negative attention she was receiving. That didn't mean I loved her.

I mean, a crush sure. She was beautiful. Funny. Confident. And she loved the boys so much. How could I not be attracted to her?

That wasn't the same thing as wanting a relationship.

We were dabbling with flirting, and there was that almost-kiss, but I couldn't risk driving her away. She was too important to Milo and Finn. I couldn't mess that up.

"I'm not in love." I paused. "I can't be."

The three of them stopped what they were doing to stare at me.

"What pathetic excuses are you coming up with?" Reese asked.

I glared at him.

"Tell us," he prodded.

"She's there for the boys. Not me. She loves them and they love her. I can't do anything to ruin that. They've been so much better with her there. They're happier, calmer, progressing again. I can't risk that."

Hartman nodded. "You're right. Things are good right now. It's better not to mess them up."

"And she's off-limits," Reese added.

"The boys' happiness comes first, of course. They would

be devastated if things *did* work out and Sydney was a permanent part of their lives. It's better to just stay away," Olli finished.

I glared back at them. "I know what you're doing."

"Just throwing some advice back in your face." Reese smiled.

Even though I had a terrible marriage and didn't find my person with Olivia, I still believed in love. I'd convinced Hartman it was okay to open himself up to Kendall and let her in. He thought he had to stay completely focused in order to be a good captain. He sacrificed everything in his personal life to make sure he didn't let anything slip on the ice. I told him to take a chance.

Reese beat himself up over his growing attraction to Chloe. Not only did she work in the front office, but she was Erik's sister. I told him to fight for her. That it was worth it.

Olli left Emma and Jackson when his depression hit an all-time low after his accident. He thought he was doing the right thing by staying away. He thought they deserved better than he could give them. It took a while, but he finally listened to me telling him they were stronger together.

My anger dissipated and I couldn't help but smile. "Who put this together?"

"It was a joint effort. There were plenty of others who wanted to come with us, but we didn't want this to turn into an intervention," Hartman answered. "You've been there for all of us for years. Now it's our turn to give the advice and make sure you don't screw up your chance."

I shook my head and stood to get some of the food. "Thanks, guys."

"Hey, your phone's ringing." Reese tossed it to me.

I didn't recognize the number and almost didn't answer in case it was a reporter, but very few people had this number.

"Hello?"

"This is Officer Lanchin. Is this Brandon Cullen?"

"Yes?" Why was an officer calling me?

"There's been an accident."

I froze. The guys started saying my name and asking questions, but their voices blurred together.

"What happened?"

"Sydney Banks was in a car accident, I believe you sons were involved as well."

"What?" I sank onto the bed. "Are they okay?"

"The boys are fine. They were taken to the hospital to be checked out."

"And Sydney?"

There was a heavy pause. "She's at the hospital as well."

"Is she okay?" I demanded.

"I'm sorry, sir. I don't know her status."

"Is she alive?" I couldn't believe I was saying these words.

"She was when they loaded her into the ambulance."

That wasn't comforting.

"What hospital?"

"The University."

"I'm in San Diego, but I'm leaving now to get there."

I hung up and raised my eyes to find them all watching me.

"Where are they?" Olli asked with his phone to his ear.

"University." I barely got the word out before a sob broke out from deep within my chest.

"What's going on? What happened?" Reese asked.

I shook my head as one tear then another rolled down my cheeks. I couldn't remember the last time I cried, but now it felt like I would never stop.

"Emma's on her way there. She'll be with the boys. She's calling the rest of the Pride. They'll take care of all three of them until we get there." Olli's words should have made me feel better, but I was pretty sure I was going to be sick.

"I have to get there."

"Our flight doesn't leave for five more hours," Hartman said before grabbing his phone. He disappeared from my view.

"They're going to be fine," Reese tried to comfort me while typing on his phone.

Milo and Finn were probably so scared. They were hurt and alone. I needed to get to my sons. I couldn't let myself think too hard about Sydney. She had to be okay. She had to be.

"Mason's letting us use his plane. It's ready to go at the airport," Hartman announced while he packed up my bag.

"Just leave it. The guys can get our stuff later." Olli offered me a hand to help me stand and in a blur, we were in the parking garage, then a SUV, then on the tarmac. A sleek white jet with San Diego's team logo was waiting for us.

"How'd you get him to let us borrow it?" Reese asked as we climbed the stairs and took our seats.

"I just had to say Cullen's boys were in an accident. He offered before I could ask."

"Huh. I guess they don't hate us as much as I thought they did," Olli said.

"At the end of the day, we're all hockey players. We're family," Hartman replied while he looked out the window.

"We'll be arriving in an hour and a half," the pilot said before shutting the door.

I stared straight ahead as we took off.

"Emma got to the hospital. They're letting her sit with the boys," Olli announced before he leaned back against his seat.

That was an immense relief, but it didn't help with not knowing how Sydney was doing.

I knew the guys were working on getting information. All I could do was focus on keeping it together. I couldn't lose it. Not until I knew.

"Do you want me to have Chloe reach out to Olivia?" Reese asked quietly after we'd been in the air for a while.

I closed my eyes. I should have thought to call her sooner. She should know about the accident, but I didn't want her to come. Not after what she'd done.

She might have a right to know, but she didn't have custody of them. She didn't get to see them unless I agreed.

"Not until we get there and we know how they're doing. I'd rather tell her they're just fine and let her video call with them than have her fly out."

"Got it."

The last thing I wanted was to see her. I could only handle so many disasters at a time.

16

SYDNEY

Pain. That was the first thing I recognized. Everything hurt. A lot. I slowly opened my eyes and realized I was in a hospital room, but why?

I tried to look around, but my neck was too sore to move.

What happened? I tried to focus on what I remembered. Picking up the boys. Snow cones. Blue and red and pink.

Fear.

Panic.

The cars. Suddenly, it came back. We were being followed. Cars with cameras aimed at us. Milo screamed. The massive SUV coming at us.

The boys! Were they okay? I needed to find them. I groaned as I tried to sit up.

"Sydney?" a voice asked.

I fought as hard as I could to move, but the pain was too much.

"You're awake." Brandon appeared over me looking concerned.

"Milo? Finn?" My throat hurt, but I couldn't relax until I knew they were okay.

Brandon reached forward and brushed my hair out of my face. "They're both fine. Emma's with them."

I closed my eyes and relaxed. They were okay. They were safe.

"How are you feeling?"

I looked up at him, too tired to lie. "Hurts."

He reached over me before leaning back. "We'll see if we can get you more pain meds."

An older woman in purple scrubs walked in. "Well, hello, Sydney. I'm glad to see you're awake. How are you feeling?"

"She said she hurts."

"Okay, I'll check and see if we can get you some more morphine for that." She disappeared, and I watched Brandon look everywhere but my face.

"Brandon?"

He paused and sighed.

"Brandon, what's wrong?" He wasn't saying something, and I needed to know. As long as the boys were safe and healthy, that was all that mattered. Was he lying about that?

"I'm so sorry, Syd. This is all my fault." The pain on his face made me cringe.

"Please don't do this, Brandon." His brows pulled together. "Don't make me say this isn't your fault. You had nothing to do with them following me. Please, don't make me."

He dropped his head. "I can't help but feel responsible."

"Don't." I was too tired to have this discussion.

"I'm sorry."

I narrowed my eyes.

"I'm sorry I wasn't there. I'm sorry you're here when it should be me."

"Stop," I said with what strength I had left. He met my eyes and finally nodded.

The nurse returned with a man. "Hi, Sydney. I'm Dr.

Stone. We're going to give you more pain meds." He picked up my chart and scanned it.

"Is this your husband?" He asked me while making a small gesture toward Brandon.

"No."

He turned to Brandon. "I'm sorry, but I have to ask you to leave."

"No, please. I want him to stay." I was scared and hurt. I didn't want to be alone.

"Fine. We had to take you in for surgery when you got here. There were signs of internal bleeding." He was avoiding my eyes. I could tell.

Brandon took my hand while we waited for him to continue.

"You took the brunt of the impact. I was told you braked, so the car hit you."

I nodded. "I didn't want the boys to get hurt."

Brandon's grip tightened.

"Well, it worked. They both have minimal injuries."

I tried to smile, but it turned into a cringe as the morphine burned through my body.

"Your pelvic bone is fractured, and there was some damage to your intestines." He still didn't look at me. "We were able to repair it, as well as the laceration to your kidney."

"What is it, Dr. Stone?" I managed to get out despite wanting to curl up and let the pain take over.

"There was more damage to your left ovary and uterus than we could repair. I'm sorry but we had to remove them."

"Everything?" I asked.

He nodded. "A total hysterectomy."

Brandon was nearly crushing my hand, but I was gripping him right back with as much strength as I could.

"Anything else?" I was terrified of the answer.

"No, you'll remain here for a few days while we monitor

you, then you'll be released but will have to remain on bed rest until your pelvis heals."

I dropped my head against the pillow and stared up at the ceiling. He continued talking about recovery, but I didn't hear anything. I just stared at the while tiles and thought about what I was going to say to my parents. Would they let me come home? After all this time?

I didn't have money for a hotel or apartment. I had nowhere else to go. How long before I could fly?

Brandon's fingers trailed down my cheek in slow, careful patterns. "It's going to be okay. We'll get through this."

"We?" I asked.

Confusion washed over him. "Yes, we. You, me, and the boys. We'll all recover together. I'll make sure you have the best nurse to take care of you."

I shook my head. "I can't watch the boys."

"I know, Syd."

"So, I'm fired."

He looked like I just slapped him. "What? Why would you think that?"

"Because I'm their nanny. If I can't watch them or take care of them, then I don't have a job."

"I'm not letting you go anywhere. I'll figure things out with the boys. The Pride has already volunteered to step in and make a schedule of who can take them. What we're all worried about is you."

I shook my head.

"Sydney, you saved my boys. You knew what you were doing when you braked. You knew you'd get hit directly. You did more than just your job. Finn and Milo love you so much. You're so good with them and they've changed so much with you around. They need you." He paused and squeezed my hand. "I need you."

"But I can't take care of them."

The corner of his lip twitched. "I don't just need you here

because of the boys. *I* need you. I can't imagine life without you. You made our house a home again. You reminded me that there can be good in my life. You're the most beautiful, thoughtful, caring woman I've ever met."

I couldn't let myself think his words meant anything more than exactly what they were. He wasn't saying he had feelings for me. There was no admission of love.

"Sydney, I need and want you in my life." He leaned down and gently kissed my forehead. "The moment I heard there'd been an accident, all I wanted was to know my sons were okay and to see you. It was the hardest thing in the world waiting to get to you. I realized how impossible it would be to live without you. I can't... I don't want to."

"Brandon." I closed my eyes. This was too much. Too close to him asking me to stay. He knew this was temporary for me. He knew this was a step toward the future I wanted.

That had changed though. Sometime over the past few weeks, this turned into more than a job or a means to an end. I wasn't waiting to leave so I could fly off to my next dream.

But that was me. That was who I was. My soul was a wanderer. I couldn't be in one spot for too long. I couldn't go from moving where and when I wanted to an instant family.

I knew one day I would leave. We all did. But why did that suddenly seem like the worst thing that could happen?

No.

No.

I couldn't give up my dream.

"Please, look at me."

I opened my eyes and blinked back the tears.

"I know we're not what you planned. I know you wanted to see the world. Live in every country. Explore and experience it all for yourself. I'm not saying you have to give that up. Just adjust it a little. See the world with me. With the boys. Every summer we can go and explore."

All of this was too much. The pain. The news. His words.

How did I go from taking the boys for a treat to lying broken in a hospital bed?

I couldn't think about what the doctor told me. It hurt too much. I'd never seriously considered having kids, but now I had no choice. That had been taken from me. Another dream I had to relinquish before it even began. How could he ask me to give up more?

"I want to be alone." The morphine was kicking in, and I just wanted everything to disappear.

His face fell, but he nodded and left.

I stared up at the ceiling tiles, trying to understand how everything could change in an instant.

Minutes or maybe hours passed before the door opened again. I didn't bother looking away from the ceiling.

"Hey Sydney," Emma's sweet voice whispered. I felt her standing next to me, but there was someone else there too.

"Hey there."

I glanced over to see Kendall's smiling face. It was crazy to think that just a handful of weeks ago she was a random barista, and Emma was a cheerful blonde I'd eavesdropped on.

"Brandon told us what happened. I hope that's okay," Kendall said carefully.

I didn't reply. I didn't care, but that was just another thing out of my control. Another thing to happen to me.

"I have no words," Emma said with a sigh. "So much was taken from you today. You did everything right. You called the police, you kept the boys calm, you sacrificed yourself for their safety. You should be getting a parade, not lying here in pain."

"I know we don't know each other well, but I can relate to the pain and frustration of being laid up in a hospital bed," Kendall said and lifted her shirt enough to show a raised scar. "I was on dialysis and nearing complete kidney failure. My life was out of my control; everything revolved around my treatment. I know it's not the same, but I wanted you to know that if you need someone to scream with about the injustice of the world, I'm here for you."

I smiled briefly. "That does make me feel better."

"Good. I know how overwhelming it is when you get bad news. It feels like the walls are closing in. It's like the future you had planned is being ripped away. You try to hold on and grasp at anything familiar. Anything you can control. I'm not telling you to give up or give in, but you will have to accept it." She grabbed my hand. "It doesn't have to define you. It doesn't have to control you, but the more you try to fight it, the more pain it causes. You have a lot of friends here who love you. We're one big, weird, dysfunctional family and you're a part of that."

Emma took my other hand. "I can only imagine what's going through your mind. I know you're a free spirit, and this may be uncomfortable or even foreign to you, but you have people here. Your people. Let us take care of you."

She was right. That was incredibly uncomfortable. I didn't feel like I was really a member of their makeshift family. I hadn't earned that. I was a loner. A drifter. Sure, I made casual friends with my coworkers or neighbors wherever I went, but once I moved, I never spoke to them again. Never missed them.

This place was different. They were sucking me in. Planting roots around my feet without my consent. Part of me wanted to sink in and let it happen, but how could I forget the dream and desire that had driven me for more than half my life?

"I don't know if I can."

Emma squeezed. "You can. You've been searching for your place. Where you belong. A home. You have that here. You have that with Brandon and Milo and Finn. With us."

"Emma, stop," Kendall interrupted. "Sydney, all we can do is tell you and show you how much we care about you. We will be here for you. We will support you and take care of you for as long as you'll have us. You've been through enough today. Just rest and know that you're not alone."

"Thank you."

She nodded and leaned lower to whisper, "Dreams change, but it has to be your choice."

"We'll let you rest," Emma said before sighing and giving me a smile. She turned then paused. "Please don't hurt them. Those three have been through too much already," she said without facing me.

It was cruel. She knew that would hit like a sledge-hammer to my heart, but it was true. When I made the decision to take the job, I opened myself to the risk of caring about them. All of them. I just never thought I would care this much.

17

BRANDON

Taking the boys home last night without Sydney was harder than I expected. They wanted to see her, and when I told them she needed to rest, they cried. Not a tantrum, mad they're not getting their way kind of cry but true sadness. It broke my heart. They really loved her, and I might have pushed her away.

I didn't want them to see her until she had a chance to let it sink in. She'd changed the moment the doctor explained her injuries.

I knew she was a free spirit. She told me her dreams of seeing the world. Her goal was to leave the country next year with an unknown return date. I tried to cage her. At the moment, all I wanted was to make sure she knew how much we cared about her. How important she was to us, but she was in her head. I could tell. She was pulling away already.

Now wasn't the time for me to give up, though. I was in this. I was committed. She might have started out as the boys' nanny, fulfilling a need my family had, but she was so much more than that now. Over the last month, she became one of us, part of our broken little family. Whether or not she could see it, she was putting us back together.

I promised the boys we'd go back to the hospital first thing this morning to see her. They kept asking to leave, but I told them they needed to eat first. They ate their breakfast without complaint. This was Sydney's doing. She reestablished rules and boundaries. Taught them what was expected and helped them learn how to behave. They no longer begged or cried to get what they wanted. Through her example of love and patience, they began to act the same.

My phone rang while I was cleaning up the kitchen. I checked the screen and almost ignored it. I had Ben, my agent, reach out to Olivia last night, but he told her not to contact me until this morning.

"Keep eating, boys. You're doing so good."

Milo smiled at me while Finn stuck another forkful of eggs in his mouth.

I went outside where I could keep an eye on them and answered. "What is it?"

"Are they okay?" At least she was getting straight to the point.

"They're fine. Milo has a few scrapes, but nothing serious."

"I'm coming."

"No, you're not," I bit out.

"You can't stop me from seeing them."

"Actually, I can. You only wanted three weeks in the summer with them, so you can wait until then."

She huffed. "They need me."

I let out a humorless laugh. "They don't. They really don't. They're doing so much better without you around."

"They're still my babies, Brandon." She sniffed for added effect.

I rolled my eyes. "You left your babies. You chose yourself and your followers over your babies. You lost the right to see them whenever you want when you decided to do that."

"You're being unreasonable. They were in a serious accident. I need to see them."

"An accident that you caused!" I shouted, then told myself to calm down. I didn't want the boys seeing me upset and thinking something was wrong.

"How is this my fault?"

Was she really so oblivious? So self-centered? "You lied, Olivia. You told the tabloids I had an affair with Sydney. That you're pregnant, and I'm denying it because of her. You put a target on her back. She was being followed by four paparazzi and hit by a fifth. They were all trying to get pictures of her and the boys. You did this."

There was a long pause before she spoke again. "I didn't know this would happen."

"Yes, you did. Every move you make is calculated. You have a team that makes every decision based on how it will impact your image and your following. You knew exactly what you were doing."

"No one on my team knew I called. I reached out to the Hollywood Times without them knowing."

Of course, she did. "Good to know I only have to sue you."

"What? Why would you do that?" The shock in her voice was apparent.

"You spread lies about me, about Sydney, and caused the accident. You will be held accountable for your actions."

"You can't do this to me, Brandon." Finally, she was getting it. She was finally realizing her actions had consequences. She never learned that while we were married, even through the divorce. Nothing clicked until now.

"My attorney will be in touch."

I hung up and leaned against the wall. How was I ever married to that monster? She hid it well when we were first together, but I should have seen the signs. She was toxic, and as much as it had killed me when she only asked for three weeks with the boys, I knew it was for the best.

Before heading back in, I sent my attorney an email asking him to take care of things with the accident and Olivia. I wanted to be as minimally involved as possible. My attention needed to be on Sydney and the boys.

I headed back inside to see the boys walking their plates to the sink. I almost stumbled over my feet at the sight. "Thank you so much, boys."

They both smiled, and Milo cocked his head. "Time to see Sydney now?"

"Yeah, we can head over."

"Yay!" They cheered and ran toward the garage. I followed them out and got them strapped into their seats.

"You guys okay?"

They nodded, and I closed the door and got in. I was relieved they weren't scared of my car or their car seats. I'd expected them to have nightmares last night, but they were handling everything like champs.

We were halfway to the hospital when Finn cried out, "Oh no!"

I nearly slammed on the breaks but managed to recover. "What's wrong?"

"We didn't make her cards," he said with sad eyes.

My shoulders dropped. Of course. We shouldn't arrive empty handed. She always made sure I had a sign or card to read before games. She was thoughtful and knew how much the boys liked it.

"You're right. We'll stop at the store and get something." I pulled into the next drug store, and we went in search of get well soon cards they liked. I also bought her chocolate and a smiley face balloon.

In the car, the boys took their time signing the card, not even needing help with their names.

"Can you write for me?" Milo asked.

I took the pen and card from him. "What do you want to say?"

"I'm sorry you're hurt. I miss you."

I cleared my throat and wrote those sweet words from him.

"Me too!" Finn handed me his card. "Write 'feel better and I miss you.'"

I obeyed and showed them both their cards for approval before sticking them in the envelopes. I didn't get a card. There wasn't enough space to say everything I wanted. How could I tell her I owed her for putting my sons' lives before her own? A simple thank you and get well soon wasn't even close to being sufficient.

No, words weren't what she needed from me. She needed to see what she meant to me, to us.

"Ready to go?"

They agreed and we arrived at the hospital a few minutes later. They proudly carried their cards and held on to the balloon together. We signed in as visitors, and then a nurse took us to her room. She was sitting up, which was a huge improvement from the day before. When she saw us, her whole face lit up. Even with dark bags under her eyes and hair that needed to be brushed, she was so incredibly beautiful. My heart ached to reach out and take her hand. To touch her and know she was okay.

"There are my favorite boys."

I wanted to believe I was included in that, but she never even glanced my way. All of her attention was on the twins.

Milo and Finn ran to her, and I had to grab their shoulders to keep them from jumping on her. "Remember she's hurt, so you have to be extra gentle."

I dropped the chocolate on her tray next to the bed and lifted the boys in my arms so they could see her better. She had some bruising on her left cheek, but overall didn't look like she'd been in a terrible accident. Her injuries were internal, which was difficult to explain to the boys. Neither of them had broken a bone, so they had no idea the pain she was in, let alone the emotional suffering I feared she was dealing with. Because of me—well Olivia and the paparazzi—she lost the ability to have her own children. That thought nearly killed me. If she'd never met me, none of this would have happened. She would be happy and healthy. She could continue to pursue all of her dreams.

"How are you feeling?"

She smiled, another improvement from yesterday. "I'm okay. The pain is much more manageable."

"And you can sit," I pointed out.

"Yeah, they have me all set up with pillows and a donut so I can sit up. I couldn't stand being on my back anymore."

"You got a donut?" Finn asked excitedly.

She laughed. "Yeah, but it's not the yummy kind."

"Aw." He pouted then seemed to remember he had a card for her. "Here, this is for you!"

Milo held his out as well. "We didn't make them, but Daddy helped us write in them."

She accepted both and smiled up at the balloon. "Thank you, guys. This makes me feel better."

She gingerly opened Finn's card and read it aloud for him. "Thank you, Finn."

She read Milo's card and reached out for the boys. I dipped them close so they could hug, but Milo took that as an invitation to climb into bed next to her. He was on her right side, but I still reached down to pull him away while also keeping Finn from jumping out of my arms.

"It's okay," she said sweetly. She situated Milo next to her then patted her other side for Finn. I helped him lay down without touching her. He nuzzled against her arm, and she turned on cartoons for them to watch while they snuggled.

I took a step back and admired how naturally they fit together. How much peace the boys got from being around her. How she seemed to need them as much as they needed her.

"They ate their breakfast without me having to remind them."

My random announcement made her smile. "That's good."

"They even brought their plates to the sink when they were done. I've never asked them to do that."

She rubbed their backs. "Good job, boys. You surprised Daddy."

They nodded without taking their eyes off the TV.

"You did that."

She glanced down. "They love learning and finding ways to help me."

"You did that, too." I pulled the chair closer to her side. "You've changed them. And me."

She finally met my eyes, looking uncertain, so I continued. "I'm not asking you to stay forever. I'm not saying you can't leave if you need to, either. I want you to know that you are a part of our family, but please don't let that scare you. I want you to come home with us. I'll make sure you have everything you need. I'll have a nurse come to help you and make sure you're healing correctly. I want you to accept my help knowing there are no expectations afterward. If you want to leave when you're back on your feet that's fine, but please let me do this for you."

She sighed and seemed to consider it. "Okay."

I'd been prepared for a long discussion, so her quick acceptance wasn't something I was ready for.

"Really?"

She smirked. "Yes, as long as you still mean it when the time comes."

Letting her go. I didn't want to, but I knew better than to try to trap her. The thought of her leaving was enough to break me. I survived Olivia leaving. I knew it was ultimately for the best. That wasn't the same with Sydney. It would devastate the boys. None of us would be the same.

"I promise."

"Okay."

She turned to look up at the TV, and I let the conversation die. Soon the boys were asleep in her arms, and I checked my phone. It was almost time for morning skate before tonight's game.

Coach Romney told me I could skip to be with the boys or Sydney if needed. I couldn't bear to leave her side, and it didn't seem like the boys were going anywhere for a while, either.

"You should go." Her voice was quiet.

I shook my head. "I'm missing the game."

"Don't."

I looked at her, and she gave me a stern look. "Why?"

"The team needs you."

"You need me."

She smiled. "I'll survive for a few hours."

"It's okay. I already talked to Coach."

"Brandon, please go. They already took enough from us. Don't let them take this game too."

I didn't want to admit she had a point, but it was true. Those leeches had done enough damage. I wouldn't be able to let it go if the team lost without me.

"Are you sure?"

She nodded.

"I'll see if I can get someone to watch the boys."

"Already done," she whispered.

There was a gentle knock on the door and Emma walked in. "Oh, this is the most adorable thing I've ever seen."

She pulled out her phone and took a picture of the boys sleeping with Sydney before looking at me. "Go. I'm here. I'll take care of them."

I smiled and stood up, giving her the chair. "Thank you."

She waved me off and sat down. I leaned over Sydney and brushed her hair back. "Promise you'll be okay?"

She nodded. "We'll be fine."

"Okay." I stared into her tawny eyes, memorizing them before stepping back. "I'll be back tonight."

They wished me luck, and I decided I'd win the game for her.

18

SYDNEY

Being back home—well, at Brandon's home—was a huge help to my sanity. After six days in the hospital, I was ready to rip my hair out. I went from one bed to another, but at least at Brandon's I wasn't being poked and prodded and woken up every few hours through the night.

It took a few days for everyone to find a rhythm and routine, but it had been a week since I left the hospital, and things were looking up. Brandon still got the boys ready in the morning and took them to preschool on his way to practice. One of the women from the Pride picked them up and either took them to a park or their house to play until Brandon was done. On the past two game nights, a group showed up to watch the game with me and keep the boys entertained. Tonight, Milo and Finn were attending with Emma and Addison.

I felt useless, but there was nothing I could do about it. Watching Brandon's community come together to help nearly made me cry every day. His teammates and their wives stepped up to help with not only the boys, but me. I felt like they'd made a schedule to make sure someone picked up the boys and arranged activities for them, but I was pretty sure they did the same for me.

At first, I tried to tell them not to worry about me, but they pushed back twice as hard. Even though I knew I was, none of them ever made me feel like a burden or obligation.

They were almost enough of a distraction from the void between me and Brandon. Even though I saw him every day, it was like there were miles between us. Sometimes he'd come and sit with me and we'd talk about nothing, but then days would go by without him even looking at me.

That hurt almost as much as my broken bones. I missed him, but didn't want to be more of a burden than I already was.

I'd had about two weeks to recover, and I was now able to stand and walk on my own. During my last check up, the doctor told me the fracture was healing faster than expected. I credited the Pride. They made sure I was able to rest as much as possible, but also made me get up, move, and stretch regularly.

"Are you ready for this?" Chloe walked into my makeshift bedroom in the living room, carrying a tray of cookies, brownies, and cakes.

"I don't think so," I said as I eyed the offering.

"I'm pretty sure I could finish that on my own," Madi announced while rubbing her belly. "This baby has given me a never-ending sweet tooth."

"Scoot over," Kendall said to Emma as she settled on the couch closest to me while reaching for a brownie.

"We've got to finish all of this before the guys get back." Addison put a few items on a plate and handed it to me.

The guys volunteered to take all the kids to dinner to give the women a break. Instead of getting dinner for ourselves, Chloe and Madi showed up with enough ingredients to start a bakery. All the guys were on a sugar-free diet until playoffs were over, so this was our chance to indulge without being glared at.

We had a few hours to watch reality TV and eat garbage without judgement, and they didn't want to waste a second of it.

"I don't get how the girls are falling for this guy. He's a wet blanket. He lets them influence him and can't stand up for himself. Sure, he's hot, but come on!" Kendall fumed while waving a peanut butter cookie around.

"They're just playing their part. I doubt any of them will actually fall in love," Addison said with her mouth full of cake.

"Where's everyone else tonight?" I'd gotten used to the rotating door of people and managed to get to know most of the women of the Pride better than I imagined.

"Amelia and Elena have a cousin visiting. Lucy and Colby went to look at wedding venues."

"I still can't believe they're leaving," Madi said with a heavy sigh. "They're not going to be around for the babies."

"They'll visit!" Emma said.

Colby and Noah were moving to Seattle this summer so he could help build the new NHL team. They said it was an amazing opportunity for him, but that didn't mean any of the women were happy about it.

"Change sucks." Addi sighed.

"It comes with the job. None of us are completely safe from leaving," Emma said.

"Well, some of us are safer than others," Addison said, giving a pointed look to Emma and Kendall.

"I have no control over that," Kendall said with her hands up. "And that's not completely true. Wyatt could get traded."

"You don't trade your captain," Madi said.

"Not Hartman, at least," Chloe added. "He's a franchise player."

"What does that mean?" I felt like they were leaving out

important details. Things they knew and understood, but I definitely didn't.

"They are players who are lifers. They become who you think of when you think of a team," Chloe clarified.

"Is Brandon one?"

They all laughed, and Kendall reached out and patted my hand. "Yes, he is. He's been with the team since he was drafted at eighteen. He's been playing at a consistent, high level for thirteen years. There's no way they'll trade him unless he asks to go."

"It's getting rarer in the NHL, but every team has those key players who stay in one place their entire career."

I knew Brandon was good. I'd seen his talent for myself, but I didn't realize it was uncommon for a player to stay where he was drafted.

"I have to hope the team stays champions, but their reign will end eventually. I think that's when changes will happen," Chloe said. "That's when Erik or Reese are at risk."

Madi sighed. "Let's not think about that. It's too depressing."

"Yes, we're all staying here forever," Addi said with finality.

I smiled at them, but knew that didn't include me. I wasn't in the same position as them. I never wanted to stay anywhere forever. They weren't like my parents, though. They didn't want to stay because of the familiarity of the location. No, it was the people. They wanted to stay with their family.

"That means you too," Chloe said as if she could read my mind.

"I don't know about that." I wanted their attention to go back to the show, but a commercial break played. No distraction there.

"I know we're not supposed to talk about it, but I have to ask. What are you going to do?" Emma asked.

"What do you mean, you're not supposed to talk about it?"

She looked around sheepishly. "Brandon told us to leave you alone to figure out what you wanted. We're not supposed to get involved."

That was sweet of him to try to give me space, but he should have known better. The Pride wasn't exactly known for observing boundaries.

"I'm not sure, yet," I answered honestly. "He said I could leave once I healed or stay until my contract is over."

"Well, obviously you can't just leave," Madi said with desperation.

I shrugged. I didn't want to talk about it. This was supposed to be a fun night of watching drama on TV, not fixating on the disaster my life was spiraling into.

"It's up to her," Chloe said while sharing a look with her sister-in-law.

"But they would be so devastated," Kendall muttered.

"Milo and Finn are stronger than we give them credit for. They'll be okay," I offered. I had to believe that. I never wanted them to get hurt. I never wanted them to feel abandoned again, but this was all temporary from the beginning.

"What about Brandon? He needs you," she argued.

"He'll find another nanny."

Emma shook her head. "That's not what she means. You weren't here. You didn't see how his ex slowly broke him down. He turned into a shell when she left. He was barely surviving. Even with all of us helping where we could, he wasn't okay. You brought him back."

"Guys, please. I was never meant to stay here long-term."

"You saved him, Syd. You reminded him he has a life to live and fight for." Chloe paused. "You told us about your parents and how important it is for you to travel. We know this was a lot to ask from you, but you completely changed their lives. I can't help but wonder if maybe they changed yours too, and you're a bit too stubborn to realize it."

That wasn't fair. I had a dream I've dedicated my entire adult life to. Then I remembered what Kendall said to me in the hospital. Dreams could change. I just had to let them.

Even considering staying felt like letting a part of myself die. World travel, being free to explore and experience all I could, had been my one and only dream for as long as I could remember. I'd sacrificed going to college, a stable career, even my relationship with my parents to pursue it.

I never regretted my decisions. I believed in fate and that everything happened for a reason. I was meant to meet the people I did and live in the places I had. Those experiences made me who I was today. I couldn't just give that up. I never met someone who understood, who felt the same pull, and I was okay with that. I truly believed I was meant to live alone as I saw the world. I wanted to eventually share my experiences in a book or blog, but in order to do that I needed to keep going. Keep moving.

How could I ever do that by staying? Brandon was a lifer here. His job controlled almost every second of his life from September to June. Would I be satisfied with just two or three months a year to travel? I didn't think so. Plus, there were the boys to consider. They were about to start school, and they needed the stability and routine of a normal life.

I didn't fit. I wasn't made for their world.

"They've helped me find a different side of me. They've shown me how much I enjoy seeing them learn and grow, but that doesn't mean I should stay. Sometimes we're only meant to experience something for a short period of time. I can take my experience here and apply it to my next chapter."

"Don't." Chloe actually sounded angry. "Don't treat them like they're just a tool for you to use and get something out of before moving on. They're a family, one you have deeply immersed yourself in. They gave you their trust. Their hearts. How can you not see that?"

How had this night turned into an attack?

"I do see that, and it's why I should leave sooner rather than later. I'm not someone for people to get attached to. It's not in my nature to stay." I shook my head. "I don't know why I have this desire, this deep need to keep moving. I just know that it's paralyzing when I ignore it."

"Maybe you're searching for something you haven't had yet," Addison added quietly.

I took a deep breath. "I think I am."

"And you still haven't found it?" Madi asked.

I shrugged. "I'm not sure."

To my surprise, they dropped it. Each of them seemed to be stuck in their heads, mindlessly snacking on the desserts and staring ahead at the TV.

I doubted any of them saw my point of view, but I didn't expect them to. They were happy. They were a part of this amazing, makeshift family. They found where they belonged.

I still hadn't.

When the guys got home, everyone was quick to leave. I said goodbye and forced a smile, but as soon as they were gone, I finally relaxed.

Brandon gave me space, but the boys wanted to sit with me until bedtime. I rubbed their backs while we watched their favorite movie for the third or fourth time that week.

"Did you guys have fun?"

They nodded.

"I missed you, though," Milo said quietly.

"I missed you, too." I shouldn't have said it. I shouldn't give any of them reason to hold onto me, but it was the truth. When they were gone, I missed them. That didn't mean I had reason enough to stay. We'd all move on eventually.

Brandon leaned against the doorframe. "It's time for bed, boys."

They sighed and started to slide off my bed, but Finn paused. "I love you, Sydney."

Milo looked between his brother and me. "I love you, too."

I smiled and told them goodnight, not daring to repeat those words back to them even though I felt them to my core.

They disappeared and I wiped under my eyes. I never expected this to happen. I didn't feel worthy of it. But their words, spoken without being prompted, gave me clarity. I knew what I had to do.

19

BRANDON

Sydney was amazing at putting on an act over the last seven weeks, but I saw through it. She improved each day, and according to her last check in, she only needed another week of bed rest.

That meant seven more days before she was free to run. I knew it was coming. I ruined things in the hospital. If there was a way for me to go back and never ask her to stay, never put that pressure on her, I would. I'd give anything to change things, to put the pieces back where they'd been before.

That was how I thought of life now. Before and after the accident. Before, when life made sense, to after, when it stopped. Before, I looked forward to each day... to after, the impending countdown pressing down on me.

I could tell her to stay. Demand that she honor the contract, but how could I hold her to anything from before?

Being here ruined her life. It took so much from her. If what she wanted was to leave, then I wouldn't stop her.

I stared down at the envelope that would give her the means to live her dream. I didn't want to give it to her. I knew it would cement her decision. It killed me to know, but watching the boys with her tore my heart to shreds. They had no idea what was coming. They wouldn't understand. They told her every day that they loved her, and she smiled and hugged them, but never said it back. I knew she did. She fell for them months ago. Maybe she was trying to protect them, but it stung.

If she couldn't say it to them, I knew she would never say it to me.

I shook my head and stood from my desk. It was time. I couldn't put this off any longer.

I walked to the living room where she was sitting up in bed. The boys were at school, and I didn't have practice until later. Now was the perfect time, if there was such a thing.

"Hey," she said as I sat on the couch next to her bed.

"I've got something for you." I held the envelope in my hands, its lightness not justifying its severity.

"Oh yeah?" She turned down the television and waited.

"Yeah, the settlement came in, and your insurance sent over the check for your car."

She nodded.

"I can find another car for you."

"That's okay." Her quick response made me sick. Of course not. She couldn't take a car with her when she left. I just wanted her to lie. To say yes and give me a glimmer of hope.

"Then this is for you."

She took the envelope from me and pulled out the first check. I wanted to throw up. It was for over a hundred thousand dollars. More than she would have made working with me in an entire year. More than she needed to fly anywhere in the world and start a new life. She could live her dream now.

"Whoa." A tiny smile pulled at the corner of her lips. She was putting it all together. "How?"

"My attorney's pretty good. None of the magazines or papers wanted to go to court, so they were happy to settle."

"Thank you." She didn't take her eyes off the check. Where she saw her ticket to freedom, I saw disappointment and pain.

"Sure, let me know if you want me to take it to your bank for you or if you need help with anything else."

I stood to leave.

"Brandon?"

I turned and forced myself to meet her eyes.

"Thank you for taking care of me."

I walked out. I tried. I took care of her. Made sure she had everything she needed or wanted. Anything I could to help her heal. We'd talk and pretend like there wasn't anything hanging over us. I fell harder. I should have let her rest, but I wanted to squeeze out every second with her I could.

A week. That's all I had left.

I wasn't giving up without a fight. I had to be able to tell the boys one day, if they asked, that I had done all I could. It would've been easier to just enjoy the days we had left, not exposing more of my heart for her to crush, but she was worth it.

It was terrifying to think of being vulnerable, even with her, but it was all I had left. It was the last play I had.

I recruited the women for help, and they jumped at the chance. Chloe and Madi were taking the boys for the night, and Emma arranged for a catered dinner, so all I had to do was focus on what I was going to say. I'd told Sydney I had dinner plans for us, but that was it. She was up and moving around much better, but I didn't want to push her by taking her out. We were going to have what I hoped was a romantic night in.

Once everything was ready, I went to the living room to help her to the dining room.

"Why do I feel like I'm walking into something scary?" she asked with a small smile.

"Nothing scary," I promised.

"Then why is everyone being so secretive."

I didn't answer, instead turning the corner so she could see the candles and flowers that I'd scattered around the room. The table was set for two.

"This is scary," she whispered as she sat and looked around.

I wasn't going to ask anything of her. I'd learned that lesson already. No, this night was my last chance to make sure she had all the cards. It wasn't time to hold anything back.

A server appeared and set salads in front of us.

"Oh wow." She smiled, seemingly impressed.

"I hope you enjoy."

She narrowed her eyes, just slightly. "What is all this?"

"It's your recovery celebration." As of today, she was officially off bed rest. The doctor warned her to take it easy, but we both knew she wouldn't stay down for long. She was restless and dying to get out of the house.

"Well, thank you. You didn't need to do all this."

"Actually, I did."

She sucked in a breath and looked away. I didn't want to ruin the meal, not yet, so I picked up my fork and quietly ate the salad. She followed my lead, and we had a careful conversation about the team and the boys. Surface level stuff.

It wasn't until she was done with the risotto that I sat up straight. "I know you're leaving, Syd."

Her eyes didn't leave her plate.

"I'm not going to stop you."

"Brandon—"

"No, just let me finish."

She sighed and leaned back.

"I'm not going to stop you, but I also can't let you leave

without knowing everything." I held her eyes while gathering the courage to say what I needed. "You know how much you mean to the boys. How much the Pride loves you. I hope you know how much I appreciate all you've done for my family, but there's one thing you don't know."

She shifted, and I knew this was pushing her, but I had to keep going.

"I love you, Sydney. I never expected this to happen when we first met. I didn't know I could feel love again, but you helped heal my heart. You gave me something to believe in. I'm not asking you to stay. I know your mind's made up, but I'm selfish and had to tell you the truth."

She clenched her jaw. "That was selfish, Brandon."

My words affected her. I couldn't help but feel a tinge of joy.

"We had an agreement. Fourteen months, then I was gone. You knew that. I was upfront with my intentions." She shook her head. "You have no right."

I didn't speak. She was absolutely right. Too bad falling for her hadn't been a choice. It happened as effortlessly as breathing. Day by day, she took a piece of my heart until she owned it all.

"You knew this was temporary for me. I was never meant to make friends with your teammates or the Pride. I wasn't supposed to fall in love with the boys. I didn't want to care about them like I do." She closed her eyes. "The thought of leaving them kills me, but I know it's for the best. The longer I'm here, the worse it's going to be because whether it's now or next summer, I'm leaving."

"But you did fall in love with boys."

"Yes, I did." She let out a breath. "It's not fair, for any of us. That's why I have to leave now."

"The boys are going to be devastated." *I* was going to be devastated.

"They're resilient," she countered. "You'll find another nanny, and they'll like her just as much."

"They already lost their mom."

She cringed. It was underhanded, throwing that in her face, but I was reaching the point of begging.

No, I needed to stop before I pushed her over the edge.

"I'm sorry," I said before she could respond. "That's not your responsibility."

She nodded. "You're right. It's not."

"I love you, Sydney." I pushed away from the table and walked out.

I said my piece. I laid it all out for her. What she did next was out of my control. I headed up to my room and crumbled onto the chair in the corner with my head in my hands. My chest was ripping in two. There was nothing I could do, and I hated it. I couldn't follow her if she left. There could be no grand gesture if she chose to walk away.

My boys, all of them, needed me here. I couldn't fly to Barcelona or Hong Kong or wherever she landed. I didn't want to reset my career, it had been too much of a blessing, but the short leash it kept me on felt suffocating at times. Like now.

I could get the twins to make her cards or tell her they loved her until she finally heard it, but I didn't want to do anything to manipulate her. It was her life and a decision she needed to be okay with. I couldn't handle her resenting us months or years from now because we used her emotions to trap her.

I was used to being in charge. Making decisions and acting on them. Staying still and letting things happen around me was one of the hardest things I'd ever done, but I loved her enough to stand back.

I didn't have the luxury of breaking down. The boys would be home soon. I had to be strong for them, especially for the next few days. They would ask about her, wonder why she left, and I would have to tell them that she loved them but had to go. Just like I did with their mom. They would cry. They would be hurt and confused. The worst part would be when they asked if they did something wrong. If she was mad at them.

It would take every ounce of strength I had to hold them and tell them they were perfect and so very loved. But I couldn't just tell them. I would have to show them. Be tough for them. Dote on them and make sure they were as happy as possible. I couldn't let myself grieve the loss of her until I knew they were okay. It might take a while, but I'd hold it together for them.

I'd tell them she was ours to love for a short time, but that she was meant to leave. To fly away.

She was a bird, and I could force her into a cage, but I wanted her to love me and the boys enough to see the cage as her home. A safe place. Somewhere she could come and go from, knowing she was always wanted. Not something to keep her limited from spreading her wings.

20

SYDNEY

Everything was in place. I arranged for Addison to pick up Milo and Finn from preschool today. She was going to take them to the aquarium and bring them home when Brandon was done with practice. Tomorrow, Emma would take them to her house to go swimming. Then it was up to Brandon to make plans.

Last night, I decided on my destination and bought my ticket to Reykjavík. I would start at one end of Europe and work my way east. I didn't have a set plan. As usual, I'd figure it out as I went. Only this time, I didn't have to panic over finding a job. I could simply enjoy the culture and sightsee. Eventually, the settlement money would run out, but as long as I was smart and frugal, I was pretty sure I could make it stretch for several years. I was putting some away in an investment account, but the rest would support me while I fulfilled my dreams.

I rubbed my hip and stared down at my empty suitcases. It had come at a cost. I was still recovering from the accident, but my doctor cleared me for normal activity. My heart would take some time to heal as well, but there were some things I'd never recover from. My choice to have children was taken away.

Over the past eight weeks I didn't let myself think about that new reality too often. Maybe it was for the best. Motherhood meant settling down. Putting someone else's needs before your own. I wasn't great at that.

I carefully folded and rolled my clothes to fit into one large suitcase and my backpack. I'd have to leave some stuff behind, but it wasn't anything I would miss. I wasn't attached to items; they were easily replaced.

The boys' faces ran through my mind, and I had to push the images away. Leaving them was the hardest part. I knew Milo would take it harder than Finn. He had a big heart, and he'd opened it for me. He let me in. He believed in me enough to trust me. He changed while I was here. I just hoped he didn't retreat back to his shell when I was gone. Hopefully he didn't blame himself. Finn would probably act out. Go back to throwing tantrums until he understood that they wouldn't get him what he wanted. One day they would forget me. They were young enough for me to become a distant memory.

Brandon was who I was hurting the most. The last thing I expected was for him to admit his feelings for me. I thought, before the accident, that there was something between us. Something that could grow, but after... I pulled away. I know I did, but so did he. We lost the connection. The spark.

He treated me like a patient, and I shut myself down.

I was hurting—physically, emotionally, and mentally. I needed him to be the one to cross the bridge. Extend a hand. Whatever. I needed him to come to me, but he gave me space. Too much of it.

Left on my own, all I could do was make plans. I had eight weeks to dream about what I would do when I could get out of that bed. Africa, South America, Europe, Asia. The possibilities were endless. I fantasized about staying a month in

Bora Bora, doing nothing but swimming and basking in the sun.

When Brandon told me about the settlement money, those dreams became real options. Wherever I wanted to go, whatever I wanted to do. I just had to take my pick.

I had plans. Goals. He knew that, but he just had to go and pull me in. He made me fall for him. I thought there was a chance before the accident. That almost kiss. I let myself hope that maybe he and the boys could be my new plan and goal. I let myself dream of a future with them. Then it all just stopped. The day he brought me home, I felt the change between us. He pulled away. He never looked at me the way he did before. He didn't touch me. Never tried to kiss me again.

Things between Brandon and me ended before they could begin, and I couldn't stand the thought of staying eleven more months knowing what might have been. I had no choice but to move on. His admission was too late.

I had accepted it.

How could he do this to me? How could he switch back and ruin everything?

I picked up a black heel and threw it against the wall.

I'm such an idiot.

I tossed the last few items in my suitcase and zipped it shut. I needed to leave. I had to get out of here. I refused to cry. I wouldn't let him get to me.

With both my bags ready, I pulled my backpack over my shoulders and headed out. I closed the pool house doors behind me for the last time and took the side path around to the front of the house. I couldn't bear to go in the main house again. This morning, I put cards on each of the boys' beds. I knew it wouldn't do much to lessen the hurt or confusion, but I was selfish and wanted them to have something to remember me by. I put my resignation letter on the desk in the office. Brandon could throw them all away later.

My taxi was already waiting for me, so I loaded my bags in the trunk and climbed in.

"Salt Lake Airport, please."

The driver nodded and pulled out of the driveway. I didn't let myself watch as we left the neighborhood. I focused all my attention on outlining the zippers on my backpack. Every thought that popped in my head was pushed out as I traced over and over.

Once we got on the freeway, I relaxed. It was a short drive to the airport, and I'd feel better once I was there. That would make it real. I could look forward to Iceland. To starting my next chapter.

My phone vibrated, and I pulled it out of the side pocket. Emma was calling. She didn't know I was leaving today, no one did, but I still didn't want to answer. I didn't want anyone trying to talk me out of this.

I silenced it and stared straight ahead.

It vibrated again and Emma's name flashed on the screen. Was it an emergency? Something with the boys?

I shook my head. They weren't my responsibility anymore.

Seconds later a text came through. *Call me asap. Chloe's in the hospital. Asking for you.*

My heart dropped. What happened to her? Was something wrong with the baby? Why was she asking for me?

We were only two exits away from the airport. I could ignore it all and just leave. There were plenty of people to take care of Chloe. She would be fine.

I closed my eyes. She'd been there for me from the beginning. She took me in, made me a part of the Fury family. She took time off work to be there for me while I recovered. She stayed at my bedside and kept me company. She encouraged me to stay strong and pushed me to get up and moving when I could. When it hurt, she told me I would get through it. That one day it would be over and I'd be stronger for it.

Could I really turn my back on her when she needed me? What kind of person did that make me?

More selfish than I was comfortable with, for one. I'd regret it forever.

"Can you please turn around? I need to get to the hospital."

The driver glanced over his shoulder. "Are you ill?"

"No, my friend needs me."

"Okay." He got off on the next exit and headed back to downtown.

I called Emma and cringed at the panic in her voice. "Are you on your way?"

"Yeah, I'll be there in a few minutes. What's going on?"

"Preeclampsia. They gave her a steroid to help accelerate the growth of the baby's lungs, and they're trying to delay inducing labor for as long as possible. It's not looking good, Syd. I think she's going to have him today."

"She's only at thirty-one weeks." I couldn't believe this was happening.

"I know. Let me know when you're here, and I'll come get you."

I hung up and stared out the window, willing the driver to go faster. I still wasn't sure why Chloe wanted me there. I had zero experience with pregnancy or birth, but it didn't matter. She was my friend and took care of me when I needed it. She didn't know anything about fractured pelvic bones—well maybe one of the guys had an injury like that before—but she also helped me cope with the reality of the hysterectomy.

I might be a wanderer, but I'd never abandon anyone. I still had four hours until my flight. If she turned out to be fine, I might be able to make it.

As soon as we pulled up to the main entrance of the hospital, I realized I'd have to lug my suitcase around, and that would raise a lot of questions.

"If I tip you really well, would you take my bag back to the house you picked me up at?" I held up two hundred-dollar bills.

He eyed them for a second and nodded. "Sure. Take care of your friend."

"Thank you!" I grabbed my backpack and ran inside. I had no idea where the labor and delivery wing was.

I called Emma and she answered on the first ring. "Are you here?"

"Yeah, where do I go?"

She walked me through the hospital until I found her at the entrance to admissions.

"You just have to sign in." I did and received a visitor's pass.

"How is she?"

"She's scared. I've never seen her like this. Reese can't calm her down, and Erik is spiraling just as much as she is."

"That's not what she needs."

Emma gave me a look that said she agreed. She looked exhausted. "How long have you been here?"

"Just an hour or so, but Jackson was up all night. He's teething again and just cries all the time."

The poor woman was dead on her feet but was still here because her friend needed her. Iceland could wait. I could wait.

"How long has she been here?"

"They came in last night around seven."

I wasn't sure what I was about to walk into, but Emma opened the door and led us in.

"There you are." Chloe was crying when we walked into the room. I went to her and took her hand.

"I'm sorry. I got here as soon as I could. Tell me what's going on?"

She sniffed. "I wasn't feeling right. My chest was pounding, and I have this horrible headache. And look." She held up her other hand. It was swollen like someone had pumped air into it. I looked at the hand I was holding and tried not to react. None of this was normal.

"So, the doctor said it was preeclampsia?" I looked to Reese and Emma for confirmation. I wasn't positive what that was, but I'd heard it mentioned before. "What does that mean?"

"Hers is pretty serious. They should have caught it when she went for her checkup two weeks ago, but according to the tests, she didn't have high blood pressure or protein in her urine. It's like it just happened overnight." Reese sounded like he was still in shock.

Erik made a sound, and I glanced over to see Madi rubbing his back. She looked just as distraught as him.

"So, can you go on bed rest or something?" There had to be a way to help her. To delay the birth.

"In some cases, but she's too high risk already. They're hoping to let the baby's lungs grow as much as possible, but if they don't deliver soon, she could have seizures or liver damage. The placenta could detach. The baby is at risk," Reese explained.

He didn't have to say anything else. I got it. Somehow Chloe went from a perfect example of a healthy pregnancy to a life or death situation.

"How long do they want to give the baby?" I asked Reese.

"The steroid takes forty-eight hours, but they don't think we can wait that long. They'll monitor to give him as long as possible, but the doctor said it will probably be in the next six hours."

That would be almost twenty hours since they came in. Hopefully their little boy was strong enough. If he was anything like his mom, he was a fighter. Too stubborn to let something like an early birth stop him.

I looked back down at Chloe and wiped away her tears.

"You can do this. Your baby has the most incredible woman I know as his mom. He's going to be okay."

She sniffed. "I'm scared."

I nodded. "I know. I was too. I didn't know if I was going to make it through the pain, but you were there with me. You told me I could do it. Now it's my turn."

It clicked why she wanted me there. Just a few weeks ago, I'd been lying in a hospital bed, crying and scared.

"This will pass." I smiled. "You told me I'd survive and I did. Now I'm telling you that you and baby boy will survive. You've got to be strong for him, okay?"

"Okay," she whispered.

I looked around the room, and Reese stepped up to the other side of Chloe's bed and rubbed her shoulder. Erik sat up straight in the chair and nodded at me. Emma came and stood next to me, putting her hand over mine.

"You have all of us here to help you, but right now you have to calm down. You've got to be strong," I said and Chloe took a deep breath. Her tears stopped and her heartbeat slowed on the monitor.

Reese met my eyes and mouthed, "Thank you."

I wasn't sure why my words helped, but somehow, they had. In this moment, I knew there was nowhere else I should be.

21

BRANDON

Word spread around the locker room when we realized Reese and Erik were missing. Olli got a call from Emma saying Chloe was in the hospital. Most of us wanted to leave and head there right away, but Coach stopped us.

"The last thing they need is the team showing up. We'll do a shorter practice, then you can check in. Give them a chance to figure things out. I'll update you as we go."

I shared a look with Olli before walking over to him. Hartman hurried over too.

"What's going on?" I asked.

"She started feeling sick last night so they went in. She has pretty serious preeclampsia."

"Oh no." I blew out a breath and rubbed my forehead.

"What? What does that mean?" Hartman looked between Olli and me.

"It means she's going to have to deliver soon," I replied.

His brows pulled together. "She's not due for like two months."

"Nine more weeks," Olli confirmed.

This was every parent's worst nightmare, but there was

nothing you could do to prevent it. You did everything you could to be healthy and careful, but it was just one of those things that happened sometimes.

"Can... can he survive?" Hartman asked quietly.

I nodded. "The twins were born at thirty-five weeks, so they were considered premature as well."

But those four weeks made a huge difference in the development of the baby. I didn't want to scare him more than he already was.

"He'll probably be in the NICU for a while," Olli said with a frown.

"Until his due date," I agreed.

"That's nine weeks." Hartman shook his head. "This is messed up."

That was one way of putting it.

"They're going to need us to stay positive. It's going to be incredibly hard, but they'll get through it," Olli said. "The child of Reese and Chloe is basically already a superhuman. He'll be okay."

I smirked. It was true. They were two of the most determined people I knew. If their baby was anything like them, he would be ready to fight.

"Let's get this over with so we can go be with them," Hartman said.

On the way through the tunnel, he took several deep breaths, and by the time he stepped onto the ice he was shouting plays and skating at full force. He was in captain mode. I shared a final look with Olli before stepping out.

It ended up being one of the worst practices we'd ever had as a team. Worse than when Olli got injured, or Erik, or even when we found out Howe wasn't coming back. None of us was focused. We were missing passes. Olli barely blocked a few shots, letting the rest in.

Finally, Coach called it.

"We'll stop wasting everyone's time. I know you all care

about Chloe and Reese. Madeline let me know that right now both mom and baby are stable. They're trying to delay labor for as long as possible, but it's likely she'll have to have him today or tonight at the latest."

Half the guys dropped their heads, some sighed, and I inched closer to the bench. I wanted to get showered, changed, and to the hospital as quickly as possible. Addison was set to pick up the boys, and I knew she would probably want to be there for Chloe too. I'd have to call her on my way.

"Let's go." Olli smacked my back as we hurried to the locker room. He, Hartman, and I were ready to leave less than ten minutes later.

"We'll get there and see what the situation is. I'll let everyone know when I have more information," Hartman told the rest of the team.

As much as Chloe and Reese loved everyone, they didn't need all twenty-plus of us showing up. Then there was the Pride. The last thing we needed to do was overwhelm Chloe.

We piled into Olli's car and were at the hospital minutes later. Emma met us at the entrance and we got signed in before heading back.

"How is she?" Olli asked before kissing his wife.

"She's doing a bit better." She glanced at me. "Sydney helped her calm down."

I froze in the middle of the hall. Sydney was here? She hadn't said anything to me, but I thought for sure she would be gone. I thought today was it.

"Come on, Brandon." Hartman waved me through the open doorway.

We crowded into Chloe's room. She was lying on the bed with monitors and wires everywhere. When she saw us, her eyes instantly teared up.

"Oh no. Come on, I thought we were done with the crying." Erik's shoulders dropped.

Chloe reached one hand up, and we took turns hugging her before surrounding the bed. I finally met Sydney's eyes. She quickly looked away and smiled at Chloe.

"See, no reason to be scared. You have half a hockey team here for you."

Chloe sniffed and giggled. She must already be on drugs because I couldn't remember the last time I heard her giggle like that. But just as suddenly as she started, she stopped. Her lower lip quivered, and I could see the fear in her eyes.

"Of course, little Murray is in a hurry to come. He wants to watch us in the playoffs," Hartman said, breaking the tension in the room.

"Impatient, just like his mom," Reese said with a half-hearted smirk.

She wacked his arm. "Erik's the impatient one."

I glanced over at her brother, and he just shrugged.

We were only able to stay in the room with her for a few minutes before the doctor came in to check on her and kicked us out. Standing across the hall from Sydney was surreal. There were hints that she was leaving today. She made sure the boys were getting picked up today and tomorrow. She hugged the boys just a little longer than normal this morning. The main thing was her inability to meet my eyes as we'd moved around each other in the kitchen.

I hadn't expected to see her again, let alone hours later.

"Syd, can we talk?"

She stared at the ground and shook her head. "Not until we know what the doctor says."

Fine, that was fair. Emma watched our exchange with narrowed eyes. I didn't tell anyone about last night's dinner. It was a mixture of pride and denial.

No one else here was aware of her plans to leave. At least, not how soon it was going to happen.

Erik paced in front of the door, clenching and unclenching his fists.

"You need to calm down. Everything's going to be okay." Madi's words didn't seem to reach him.

He just kept going back and forth until the door opened and the doctor stepped out. He nodded once at us before walking away, and we flooded back into the room.

Chloe looked stunned, and Reese's face was white.

"What's going on?" Erik demanded.

"It's time," Chloe announced.

"What? I thought you had a few more hours," he argued.

"The baby is showing signs of distress. They don't want to wait for him to get critical," Reese explained.

"Are they doing a C-section?" I asked.

Chloe nodded silently.

The women moved to surround her, whispering.

I moved to Reese. "This is a good thing. Your baby will be out in just a few minutes and they can start treating him and work on getting Chloe healthy again."

He nodded, but he still looked terrified.

"You're about to become a dad." I squeezed his shoulder. "Don't let fear take this moment away from you."

He met my eyes and smiled. "You're right."

A nurse walked in and told us it was time to take them, so we moved out of the way. For several moments, no one spoke.

Erik fell back onto the chair. "Our parents should be here. They would know what to say to make it better."

Madi wrapped her arms around him. "They're here. They're watching over her and baby boy."

I felt like I was interrupting a moment, so I slipped out of the room. Olli, Emma, and Sydney followed. She walked past me and glanced over her shoulder. "Come on."

We ended up at the end of another quiet hall. She stopped and crossed her arms over her chest. I didn't know what to say. I had no words left.

"Emma called and said that Chloe wanted me here," she

said to the ground. "I tried to tell myself she had enough people to take care of her. Whatever was going on, she didn't need me." She shook her head. "It took me about two seconds to realize that even though it was true, it didn't matter. Chloe's my friend, and she wanted me here. After all she's done to help me, how could I possibly say no?"

She finally looked at me. "I'm not a bad person. I don't desert people, especially when they need me."

I was tempted to argue that, but she kept going.

"From the moment we met, she accepted me. She stood by me when I needed someone the most. She never once let me down. I didn't have a choice. I had to come."

"But you have a choice with me and the boys?" I was trying to understand, but it felt like she was speaking in code.

"You were changing my mind, Brandon," she rushed out. "Before you left. Before the accident happened. I thought." She shrugged. "I thought about staying."

"So, what changed?" I asked the one thing that had been bothering me for weeks.

"You pulled away." The disappointment in her voice was a punch to the gut.

"You were hurt. I was letting you heal."

She sighed. "Chloe, Emma, and Addison—women I barely knew from the Pride—came every single day. They kept me company, they told me to push through and not give up, they were there. Every. Single. Day."

"So was I."

She shook her head. "No, you might have been in the house, but you could go days without looking me in the eyes. Without even coming into the room."

I fell back against the wall. "It was my fault. Everything was my fault. I couldn't look at you. I couldn't see what I'd done without breaking down."

She took a step closer to me, straightening as she shoved

her finger into my chest. "You had nothing to do with it. You weren't driving the car. You weren't there."

"But none of it would have happened if you hadn't come into my life."

She let out a huff and stepped back until she was against the opposite wall. "You're right. *None* of it would have happened. I wouldn't have gotten to know the boys. I wouldn't have fallen in love with them. I wouldn't know you. Or the Pride. My life wouldn't have changed at all." She sniffed. "But it did. It did happen, and I wouldn't take a second of it back."

"Then why are you leaving?" I pleaded.

"Because you left." Her voice broke. "When I needed you the most, you left."

I rubbed my hands over my face. "I was right there. The whole time. I was there for you. I was giving you space to come to me."

She narrowed her eyes. "I was bed ridden. Scared. Coming to terms with how quickly my life changed. You turned into a ghost."

We were talking in circles. Neither of us was willing to concede. If I wanted her to stay, it was time to fight.

"I'm sorry."

Her shoulders sagged. "Me too."

"Please, don't go. I meant what I said. I love you, and I want you in my life. I want you in the boys' lives."

She flinched. "I can't."

"Yes, you can. It's not too late for us." I was ready to get on my knees and beg. This was the second chance I never thought I'd get. I couldn't hold back. "I'm so sorry for letting you down. I will never stop making it up to you. It was terrifying for both of us, and I realized how much the possibility of losing you hurt. It nearly broke me. When you came home from the hospital, I didn't know what to do or say. I was still so scared. I wasn't there for you like I should have been, but I promise I will never let that happen again. I will always be there for you. I will love and support you forever. I will take you around the world. I will make sure you have all the adventures and experiences you could ever dream of." I swallowed. "Just please don't leave."

She didn't say anything. No refusal. I took slow steps toward her and lifted her hands into mine. "I love you, Sydney Banks. Please give me another chance."

She looked up and it felt like she was searching my soul. She opened her mouth, and Emma came rushing toward us.

"He's here."

Syd pulled her hands away and followed Emma down the hall.

22

SYDNEY

C hloe had improved considerably by the time visiting hours were over. They didn't have a name for Baby Boy yet, but he was doing better than we could have hoped.

His lungs were more developed than the doctors expected, but he was still taken directly to the NICU and hooked up to what seemed like a hundred tubes. He was the tiniest thing I'd ever seen. He weighed three pounds, six ounces.

We were only able to look in on his incubator before having to leave. Reese stayed with him while Erik and Madi stayed with Chloe.

I loved the way everyone pulled together for them. Seeing more and more of the team arrive with their wives nearly brought me to tears. This was their family. They were so lucky to have such an amazing group to love and support them.

As I walked back to my car, I froze in the middle of the main lobby. My heart ached at the thought of losing this. For a moment, I was a part of this Fury family. Was that what I wanted? Was that what I had been searching for these past ten years?

Maybe it wasn't the adventure and memories I was chasing. Maybe it was a sense of belonging. A family that truly understood and accepted me. My parents never did. They couldn't imagine anything bigger than their quiet life.

The Pride and the Fury? They got it. They knew how to dream big and achieve their goals. Each one of them was more driven than the next. They were risk takers, travelers, but mostly they had wide open hearts.

Milo and Finn accepted me, all of my quirks and new ideas and discipline. They allowed me into their lives, made room for me in their battered hearts. They had no reason to trust me, but they did. They could have acted out, thinking I would hurt them like their mom did. I would have understood, but those sweet boys loved me instead.

How could I leave them?

Brandon's pleas ran through my mind over and over. He was in love with me. He wanted me to stay. He wanted to be included in my dreams.

Why was I pushing him away?

I hurried outside then and realized I had nowhere to go and no way to get there.

"Need a ride?" A voice behind me called.

I spun and saw Brandon's car parked near the entrance. Of course, he was here.

For someone who firmly believed in fate, I was sure running from the signs. First, Emma called me just before I got to the airport. Now, when I needed him the most, Brandon was there.

I walked over to his window, stopping a few feet back. "Get out."

He hesitated before opening the door and stepping toward me.

"When you pulled away from me, I thought it meant you

didn't care about me anymore. I thought your feelings changed." I paused to keep the emotion out of my voice. "I was scared, so I pulled away too. I decided to do what I'm best at. Moving on without looking back."

"I'm sorry." He took a step forward.

I held up my hand. "I know. I'm sorry too. I shouldn't run away. That shouldn't be my default, but I was trying to protect myself. I've always put myself first. This is new territory for me."

He nodded. "I know."

"I wasn't prepared to like them, let alone love them. I wasn't expecting to change so much in such a short period of time. I never, ever thought I'd fall in love with you."

He took another step forward, and this time I didn't stop him. "You can't control everything."

I shook my head. "No, I can't."

"Sometimes you have to let life happen." He stopped inches away from me.

"I know." My heart raced.

He reached out and took my hands in his. "I'll never try to stop you from exploring and traveling. Being with me, with the boys, isn't a prison. It might have felt that way lately, but I promise I won't try to contain you."

Living in one place, establishing roots, finding a family wasn't the same as giving in. It wasn't accepting the same life my parents had. I could still be me, be a free spirit, and be happy.

"It's not going to be easy," I warned.

He lifted my right hand and kissed it. "It's not going to be as hard as you think."

"I'll get restless."

He repeated his kiss on my left hand. "We can keep up."

"I'm not normal."

His lips curved into a breathtaking smile. "None of us are."

"I love you," I whispered just before his lips captured mine. There was nothing timid or cautious about this kiss. One hand snaked around my waist, pulling me closer, while the other threaded through my hair holding me exactly where he needed me.

There were promises made with each nip and peck. We were in this together. We wouldn't pull away ever again. Our love was enough.

"I love you, Sydney." His voice was low in my ear.

I dropped my forehead against his chest. Brandon Cullen, the dad, the hockey player, the man of my dreams, loved me.

"Let's go home," I said.

He pulled back. "Say that again."

I grinned up at him. "Let's go home. I want to see our boys."

His eyes softened, and he kissed my temple. "Let's go home."

He opened the car door for me and we drove in silence, holding hands and soaking in the moment.

Addison's car was in the driveway and when we walked in, and she eyed us before picking up Jackson. "I told the boys they could play for a few minutes before bed." She stared down at our joined hands and smiled before wishing us a good night and leaving. I wondered for a moment if she knew, but it didn't matter. I was here, and I wasn't going anywhere.

"Come on."

When we got to the top of the stairs, I dropped his hand and hurried into their bedroom. The cards I made were still waiting on their pillows, so I grabbed them and tossed them in the bathroom trash can before meeting Brandon in the hall.

"What were those?" he asked.

"Nothing that matters anymore."

He hesitated, but didn't say anything and walked down to the playroom. "Hey, guys."

I followed behind him and nearly cried when the boys saw us. Their excitement was so obvious.

"Daddy! Sydney!" They ran over and wrapped their arms around our legs. I bent down, basking in their hugs.

"I missed you, guys." I kissed the top of their heads while they giggled.

"You saw us this morning," Milo said.

"I know." I smiled and took his hand. "Are you guys ready for bed?"

Finn skipped ahead of us to their room. Brandon and I settled them in, and when I went to give each of them a hug, I whispered something I wouldn't let myself say before now.

"I love you."

Want more hockey romance with a second chance at love?

In Power Play, Jason pays for the mistakes of his past and earns back Taylor's trust.

You'll also get more of Brandon and Sydney's story as the Utah Fury Hockey Series continues.

Keep reading for a sneak peek into their story.

Thanks for reading! I hope you enjoyed Brandon and Sydney's story!
Word of mouth is so important for authors to succeed. If you enjoyed Penalty Kill, I'd love for you to leave a review on Amazon!

Keep Reading,
Xoxo B

SNEAK PEEK: POWER PLAY

CHAPTER 1

Taylor

Sleep deprivation was messing with my head. It had to be. There was no way I was twenty miles from Nashville. That was in the opposite direction of where I was supposed to be going. My heart rate picked up when I saw another sign announcing the split toward Nashville. I wasn't hallucinating. I really was in Tennessee.

I pulled off on the next exit and into the nearest gas station. I picked up my phone and checked the map. Oh no.

No.

No.

No.

No.

Somewhere, who knew how long ago, I'd taken a wrong turn. A wrong freeway. I'd been on this one for hours. Since ... Louisville.

Wait. Louisville? Why had I been anywhere near Kentucky?

Detroit to Columbus. Southwest, straight through West Virginia.

No. Southeast.

I dropped my head against the steering wheel and fought back tears. There was no use in crying. That wouldn't help anything, and I'd end up with a headache.

How could this have happened? I went over my route at least a hundred times before leaving. Carrie, my older sister, had me repeat it back to her twice before I got in the car. Sure, I'd been engrossed in the audiobook I'd been listening to and was mostly on autopilot, but not enough to end up in the wrong state!

I didn't have time to panic. I had to fix this. I set my destination as Raleigh in my phone's GPS and swallowed back the lump that formed. Over eight hours away.

It was two in the morning, and I was due to start my new position with the Pugston Firm at eight-thirty. The most prestigious accounting firm on the East Coast, outside of New York City, and I royally screwed it up. I wrote an email explaining the situation and sent it to my contact, the human resources director, but I doubted any excuse was valid for missing my first day. They could hire anyone they wanted. They probably had a list of excellent candidates they could call and replace me with before I even made it to the city.

I wouldn't know until she arrived at the office in the morning, so I had to push through. Giving up was not an option, not when there was still a scrap of hope.

I bought two energy drinks before getting back on the road. Eight more hours of driving. I could do it.

The email came in at eight-fifteen. I glanced at the message long enough to see "We regret to inform you ..." I pulled off and read the full email. They rescinded their offer and wished me luck. Of course, they did. Why on earth would they want someone so absent-minded and incapable working for them?

I had nowhere to go. Nowhere to be. Returning home was too humiliating to be an option. Not after my family bragged to everyone they knew about my big fancy job. I couldn't show my face again until Christmas.

Less than two hours to Raleigh. I sighed and got back on the road. I had a hotel room waiting for me, and I was too tired to think of a better plan at the moment. Once I got there and slept for a few hours, I would come up with the next steps.

I shuffled into the lobby with my two suitcases and leaned against the counter.

"How may I help you?" The woman eyed me with a fixed smile. Her perfectly sleek bun and impeccable makeup was a reminder that I hadn't showered in two days. Her judgment was too far down on my list of concerns for me to care.

"I have a reservation under Taylor Klein."

She tapped on the keyboard and frowned. "I'm sorry but your check-in isn't until three this afternoon."

Right. Because I was supposed to be at work right now and check in tonight. "I've been driving for two days. I know I'm a bit early but surely you have a room available. Could you please check?" As much as I wanted to cry or scream at her, I knew I'd get further by being polite. Something my parents taught me.

Her fake smile returned, and she clicked on her mouse a few times. "We are quite full this week, but it looks like I have a room with a queen available."

"That would be great. Thanks for checking." I slid my ID and credit card toward her.

It seemed to pain her to be nice to me, but she handed me my things along with a keycard. "You'll be in room two-twelve. Enjoy your stay."

"Thanks." I smiled and turned to find the elevators.

The moment I opened the door to my sanctuary, I dropped my bags and collapsed onto the plush bed. Tears rolled down my cheeks, and this time I didn't have the strength to stop them. This was supposed to be my moment. All my hard work and sacrifice seemed to pay off when I got such an amazing offer. It had been sudden. They wanted me to start just three days after I accepted the job. There wasn't much time to prepare for my life down here. I just packed up and my parents said I could figure things out when I got here. Ask my coworkers for recommendations of where to live and take time to find the neighborhood that felt right. After all, this was the beginning of the rest of my life.

I had budgeted for a hotel room for a week to give me time to find somewhere permanent to live, but now I would probably need to move again. The last thing I wanted was to ask my parents for help, not after how proud they'd been. I would do this on my own.

H unger was the only motivation strong enough to get me to wake up and move. I managed to sleep for seven hours but was still so exhausted. It was after five, and I could've easily continued sleeping through the night but my stomach grumbled. Once I stood, though, I realized how desperately I needed a shower. I could smell myself. My pride--and my mother's voice--prevented me from seeking out food without bathing first.

Once I was presentable, I took the stairs down to the main lobby and found the concierge's desk.

He grinned as I approached. "Good evening, Miss. How may I help you?"

"I'm looking for a recommendation for somewhere close to get dinner."

He pulled out a list and a map before pausing. "Are you a Storm's fan?"

I had no idea what he was talking about. Did I like storms? I shook my head.

"Then might I suggest Hillsborough Sports Bar. It has a full dinner menu as well as a superb selection of craft beers. It's just across the street and down half a block." He raised his hand to the left.

"Thanks so much." I smiled and headed in the direction he pointed. I saw the neon signs easily and nearly ran. I was hungrier than I thought, and knowing food was within reach, I didn't bother to care if people saw me rushing down the sidewalk.

I stepped through the front door and was pleased to see it was more restaurant than bar, with sports memorabilia covering every flat surface, surrounding the wide-open area of tables that were mostly full. I forced my way through the mass of people to the front. A hostess greeted me, and when I said I was alone she recommended a seat at the bar for quicker service. A forty-minute wait to sit at a booth wasn't worth it.

I found a single open stool and the bartender nodded in acknowledgment while taking the order of a man down at the opposite end.

There was a small, folded menu standing between the salt and pepper shakers and napkin holder, so I pulled it out and scanned the options. A juicy burger sounded like heaven. My mouth watered at the thought of dipping salty fries in ranch.

With my mind made up, I replaced the menu and waited for the single bartender to make his way down to me.

A dozen or so TVs made up the entire wall behind the shelves of bottles. Each one displayed a different sporting event or commentator. A few of them were discussing the same hockey game. I cringed and looked away.

"Sorry about the wait. What can I get you?" The bartender shifted back and forth on his feet like he couldn't possibly stand still.

"The All-American Burger, fries with a side of ranch, and a water to drink, please." Something stronger was tempting, but I'd been cruel enough to my body the past few days. The best thing I could do was rehydrate so I had a clear head tomorrow. That's when I would face my problems and figure out what to do next.

He nodded, picked up a glass, and began to fill it. "I'll get that right up." He placed the water in front of me and moved to a computer screen at the far corner of the bar.

I looked around, taking in the décor, and paused on a row of jerseys. North Carolina Storm. That's what the concierge meant. Was I a fan of their hockey team? Why would that matter? My attention went back to the screens, and I found a set of commentators discussing the upcoming finals. The Stanley Cup was taking place.

I read the closed captioning as the pieces fell into place. The Storm were in the finals, and the first game of the series was tomorrow. In Raleigh. No wonder the hotel was so busy, and the wait was so long here. But if I wasn't a Storm fan, why did he send me here? I twisted in my seat and casually scanned the room as if looking for someone.

Oh no.

Could I still blame sleep deprivation for this oversight? I was in a sea of black and maroon. Utah Fury fans. Everywhere.

I faced forward and hung my head. Maybe if I hadn't been so wrapped up in graduation, interviews, and moving out, I would have realized sooner what was happening. According to the TV, the Storms hadn't been to the finals in decades. The city was celebrating and fans of their opponents, the Fury, were arriving in droves.

Great. I wasn't going to be able to escape this. Everywhere I looked, there were reminders.

The universe was obviously trying to teach me a lesson. I wasn't sure what it was, but there was no other explanation for the crapshoot my life had become. Missing my first day of work, losing my dream job, sitting in a crowded restaurant in a city where I didn't know a soul, and now the stupid hockey celebration was slapping me across the face.

There was only so much a person could handle before crumbling, and I was toeing that line.

"Here you go." A plate slid in front of me but I barely got out a thanks before the bartender moved on. I kept my eyes down, forcing myself to take small bites of food. I lost my appetite in my wave of self-pity, but I knew I would end up sick if I didn't get something down.

If I was going to fix this tomorrow, I needed to take care of myself now. I didn't have to think yet. No pressure. Just bite, chew, swallow, and repeat.

The tears threatened to make another appearance, but I closed my eyes and fought them back. I would not lose it in public. I didn't look around, not even to the TVs. My only goal was finishing as much as I could and getting out of there. I could hide in my room and forget the outside world, at least for a few days. I didn't have enough money in my account to stay long, not without a job.

Another wave of desperation hit. I couldn't do anything right then. I just had to finish my meal. Then I could freak out.

The energy in the restaurant shifted without warning. I raised my head and looked around. The area near the front doors had fallen silent. I watched with those around me as a group of men, followed by two women, emerged from outside and walked directly toward the bar. The ten or so of them were laughing and chatting, seemingly oblivious to the effect they had on the people in the restaurant.

A few of them wore hats pulled low over their faces, but they were all dressed casually. They were good-looking, but not enough to silence a crowd. I didn't recognize anyone whose faces I could see as famous so I turned back around in my seat and took a sip of water.

"Not much of a fan?" The bartender was standing in front of me, although his eyes were trailing the men walking behind me.

"No, not really." Once I was, but definitely not now.

"If you're not in town for the game, what brings you here?" he asked.

It seemed strange for him to be making small talk with me since he hadn't paused on any one person for longer than a few seconds since I sat down. Then I realized he was still watching the men who had settled at a large table behind me, and I must be sitting at his best view.

"I was supposed to start a job this morning, but I took a wrong turn in Ohio, at least I think it was Ohio. Anyway, I missed my first day and they fired me. So, I'm in a new city where I don't know anyone and don't have a job."

His eyes flickered to mine. "You sure I can't get you anything else to drink? On me?"

I smiled and shook my head. "No, thanks though."

A laugh I recognized sounded behind me, and my stomach dropped. Nope. It couldn't be him. I glanced over my shoulder as his unmistakable voice rose above the others. Heat—a raw rage—washed over me.

I turned back around. "Actually, could I get a glass of your cheapest red wine?"

The bartender found a bottle and poured a generous serving before setting it in front of me.

"Thank you." I smiled and picked it up by the stem. My entire body shook as I stood.

I hadn't been this angry in years. Not when I realized my mistake this morning. Not when I lost the job. Oh no. This was next-level fury. I almost laughed at the irony.

"Miss?" I heard the bartender call after me, but I ignored him and took slow, determined steps toward my target.

Four years. It had been four long years since I heard that voice. The one that used to make my heart sing. The one that promised me so much only to disappear from my life right when I needed him most.

There he was. None of them looked up as I approached. He looked the same. Unfortunately. He was just as handsome as the last time I saw him. Thick dark hair, a jawline that could make supermodels cry, and those shoulders. Only it was all wrong. His hair was longer under his hat. There was scruff on his face. His shoulders were wider than I remembered. He was a man now.

I stopped across from him and waited as he glanced up, did a double-take, and dropped his mouth.

That caught the attention of one of the guys. He called his name and nudged him. Soon, the entire table was watching him.

"Taylor?"

I flung my hand up, aiming the wine at his face. I hit my target and spun back around without a word.

Continue reading Power Play now!

ALSO BY BRITTNEY MULLINER

ROMANCE

Utah Fury Hockey

Puck Drop (Reese and Chloe)

Match Penalty (Erik and Madeline)

Line Change (Noah and Colby)

Attaching Zone (Wyatt and Kendall)

Buzzer Beater (Colin and Lucy)

Open Net (Olli and Emma)

Full Strength (Grant and Addison)

Drop Pass (Nikolay and Elena)

Scoring Chance (Derrek and Amelia)

Penalty Kill (Brandon and Sydney)

Power Play (Jason and Taylor)

Center Ice (Jake and Dani)

Game Misconduct (Parker and Vivian)

Face Off (Mikey and Holly)

Snowflakes & Ice Skates (Lance and Jessica)

A Holiday Short Story to be read between Center Ice and Game Misconduct

West Penn Hockey

Cheat Shot

Trick Play

Enemy Games

Fake Assist

Royals of Lochland

His Royal Request

His Royal Regret

Her Royal Rebellion

Young Adult

No Regrets Series

Ask No Questions

Tell No Lies

Make No Mistake

Charmed Series

Finding My Charming

Finding My Forever

Standalones

The Invisibles

ABOUT THE AUTHOR

Brittney Mulliner writes contemporary, young adult, and sports romance novels for readers of all ages. As a life-long avid reader, growing up, her parents would often take away her books to make her go play outside, but nothing could compare to the adventure of a good book. Born and raised in Southern California, she now lives in the Rocky Mountains with her husband and Goldendoodle, Freddie Mercury. She's a devout hockey fan, loves working out while listening to audiobooks, and is on a lifelong hunt for the best gluten-free cinnamon roll.

For exclusive content and the most up to date news, sign up for Brittney's newsletter here.

Find out more about Brittney and her books at
www.Brittneymulliner.com

Made in the USA
Columbia, SC
09 August 2022

64540462R00126